W9-DFM-036

COMING NEXT IN THE DALE HUNTER SERIES OF NOVELS:

Simply the Best

"It may be simple, it's never easy."

(1st Chapter at the end of this book)

Merger Maniac

"Some offers have to be refused."

Bad Boys in Boston

"It's just business, never personal."

Crash Landing

"Public pressure, private pain."

Also by Del Chatterson,

writing for entrepreneurs as Your Uncle Ralph,

The Complete Do-It-Yourself Guide to Business Plans

"It's about the process, not the product."

Don't Do It the Hard Way

"A wise man learns from the mistakes of others,
Only a fool insists on making his own."

You never win playing by the rules...

Shelagh!
Thank you!
Enjoy the
adventure!
Del.
28 Sept. 2019.

NO EASY MONEY

DELVIN CHATTERSON

© 2018
Delvin R. Chatterson
All rights reserved to 146152 Canada Inc.

Disclaimer: Some of the events, individuals and companies in this book are real, but the story and the primary characters are entirely fiction. Any apparent use of real names or similarity to real people is purely coincidental.

Credits:
Money for Nothing by Dire Straits, written by Mark Knopfler and Sting, Album *On the Night* © 1993 Phonogram Ltd. (London)
Edited by Alan Rinzler, Berkley CA and Allister Thompson, Ontario, Canada. Cover design by Caroline Teagle, New York, NY. Author photos by Mario Carangi, fotovation, Montreal, QC.

Published by:
Uncle Ralph's Publishing Empire
(Division of 146152 Canada Inc.)

&

Tellwell Talent
www.tellwell.ca

ISBN
978-0-22880-482-6 (Hardcover)
978-0-22880-483-3 (Paperback)
978-0-22880-481-9 (eBook)

Dedicated to enlightened entrepreneurs everywhere,
trying to do better for themselves and their families,
their employees, customers and suppliers,
their communities and the planet.

Also dedicated to the families, friends
and lovers of entrepreneurs.

LOOKING BACK

Money for nothing and the chicks are free

Dale Hunter was stuck in the continuous congestion of the Decarie Expressway driving toward downtown Montreal and that line was stuck in his head.

He was a fan of Dire Straits and their hit song, "Money for Nothing" was on the radio. His favorite was "Sultans of Swing" with Mark Knopfler's long guitar solo at the end, though the DJs always let it fade out before the solo run was over.

"Money for Nothing" reminded him of the 1980s and the computer business he owned back then. *A nice idea*, he thought, *but the money is never for nothing. Never has been for me anyway.*

It was a hot, humid day in July and Dale cursed himself for getting caught in the rush hour traffic. Now that he was retired, he should have been able to avoid it. He would rather have been cruising in his BMW M4 with the top down along a winding road in the Laurentian Mountains away from the city. Instead, he was jammed into a pack of Montreal drivers with the top up and the windows closed, the air conditioning straining to shut out the heat, noise and pollution of the six-lane concrete trench known as the Decarie. It was always a stressful drive, so the music was a useful distraction and the old favorites were added relief.

His mind wandered back thirty years, to the time when Dire Straits first recorded those hits and he was a young entrepreneur riding high on the wave of personal computers that were flooding across North America. He smiled at the memories.

Then Dale remembered the first time that Jacques Talbot walked into his office and life became more difficult and more dangerous. The smile faded.

Talk about money for nothing.

1.

It was a cold winter day in January 1986, the day after the Space Shuttle Challenger had exploded immediately after take-off from Cape Canaveral, killing all seven astronauts. Everyone was talking about it. The TV images of shocked spectators looking up at the lingering brown plumes of smoke drifting away against a clear blue sky would be etched into their memories forever.

Dale Hunter was in his office in Montreal working on his own launch for a new line of computer products. He was writing up the promotions and product announcements to give to his sales team at 3D Computer Products.

Lost in thought staring at the computer screen, he was interrupted by his receptionist, Marie de Carlo, as she stepped into his office.

"Dale," she said, "There's somebody here to see you about insurance."

"Insurance?" He didn't turn from his keyboard. "I don't need to see anybody about insurance."

He heard a deep French-Canadian man's voice.

"But Mr. Hunter, this is a very special kind of insurance. I'm sure it will be good for your business."

The voice was coming from the doorway behind his startled receptionist.

Dale looked up to see a heavy-set man in a grey suit, no tie. An unfriendly face with an insincere smile. His hair was slicked straight back and down to his collar. Shiny black biker boots with rubber soles had allowed him to silently follow Marie down the hall.

"Thank you, miss," he said, as he squeezed by Marie, stepped into the office and reached out to Dale for a firm handshake.

He took a chair and pulled it up close to Dale's desk. Marie disappeared back down the hallway.

"My name is Jacques."

Dale took another look at him. *No last name, no business card? Not your typical insurance salesman.*

His suit fit tightly around heavy arms and shoulders. A burgundy silk shirt exposed gold chains at his neck and was stretched tightly over his round belly. *La grosse bedaine* as they say in Quebec.

If I ever have a big belly like that, thought Dale, *please just shoot me.*

"I really don't need any insurance," Dale said. "We're well covered and I don't have time right now to hear your pitch. Leave me your card and I'll call if I'm interested. Thanks anyway, but I don't want to waste your time or mine."

"Mr. Hunter," Jacques said, as he leaned forward holding the thin smile. "You don't seem to realize, this is insurance you absolutely must have. It's not really negotiable."

"Not negotiable... How's that?"

"Well, if you do business with us, we guarantee that certain types of accidents will just never happen." Jacques's smile disappeared and his eyes turned dark and menacing.

"And if you *don't* pay our insurance, we can promise you *will* have an accident. Either here or at home." He sat back and let it sink in.

"Jesus! You're looking for protection money?"

"We prefer to call it insurance."

Dale's mind raced and his stomach clenched as a cold chill ran down his back. He jumped up and pointed at the door.

"Get the fuck out of here or I'm calling the cops, right now."

Jacques looked up, not moving from the chair. The smile returned. He continued, speaking slowly and firmly.

"That's never a good idea. Our insurance actually protects you better than the cops and we really don't want them interfering in our business. This arrangement is just between us."

"We don't have an arrangement. So just get out of here, now!"

Jacques ignored him and continued.

"If I hear anything about cops, two things will happen. First, we'll show you the kind of accident that we're protecting you from, and second, your insurance will double from one thousand a week to two."

"No bloody way!"

"Look, I know you weren't expecting me today, so I'll give you some time to get used to it. I'll come back tomorrow afternoon. Just be sure you have an envelope ready for me. Mark it "Guaranteed Insurance" and put a thousand cash in it. Very simple. Got it?"

Dale glared at him and said nothing. Jacques got up and left the office.

Dale sat back stunned, then slammed his hand on the desk and exploded.

"Sonofabitch! Where the hell did he come from?"

Marie came back down the hall from her reception desk after Jacques went out the front door and looked in on Dale.

"Everything all right?" she said. "Who was that guy?"

"Uh, yeah, no problem. Just another high pressure salesman."

"Oh, OK." She went back to the front desk.

I need to have the cops here waiting for the sonofabitch when he comes back tomorrow, Dale was thinking. *I need to stop this before it goes any further.*

Then he heard a crunch and the sound of broken glass coming from the parking lot. He stood up and looked out to see a red Dodge RAM pickup backing away from the rear of his grey BMW coupe. The truck pulled forward to the curb alongside the building. Jacques got out and headed back in the front door.

He walked past Marie with a quick glance that froze her in place and went straight on to Dale's office. She watched him go down the aisle between the desks against the windows and the closed offices along the facing wall. The sales rep, Sylvie Cloutier, looked up from the paperwork on her desk and frowned as he went striding by.

Jacques went straight through Dale's doorway, walked over and leaned across the desk into Dale's face.

"I had the feeling you might still be thinking about calling the cops."

He stood back with his hands on his hips and fingers below his belly. The grey suit jacket was pulled back like a gunslinger ready for a shoot-out.

"I decided to give you a small demonstration of how we work. Just a broken tail-light this time, but if you ever go to the cops, we'll have to do more damage." He stepped forward to put both hands on Dale's desk and lean over it again.

"Remember, we know where you live and where your kids go to school. They're really cute in their little uniforms at Kirkland Academy. Don't give me a reason to run into them next time, instead of your car. Have the cash ready tomorrow."

Dale stared at him and sat still, trying to suppress the shudder that shook him in his chair.

"Just pay your insurance and I'll include child protection, no extra charge." Jacques smirked.

"See you tomorrow."

He turned and left again.

The back of Dale's neck tingled as he held his head in his hands, elbows on the desk.

This is for real.

He reached out and absent-mindedly straightened the blotter to line it up with the front edge of his desk. Then he aligned the flat leather coaster with the top edge of the blotter.

Dale got up and went to the door, closed it quietly, then paced slowly between the windows and the book case, circling the small conference table and two chairs. He paused to straighten a book on the shelf and stooped to arrange the papers more neatly in the blue recycling bin by his desk, then continued pacing.

It was a nervous habit. He was aware of it, but denied that he had what some people called OCD.

"I'm neither obsessive nor compulsive and it's not a disorder," he explained. "I'm just trying to bring a little order into the chaos around me."

The visit from Jacques, demanding protection money and threatening his family, was going to be a challenge to bring into order.

2.

Dale was not an experienced entrepreneur. He had started his company, 3D Computer Products, only two years earlier, after a painful exit from the corporate world.

He had been working with an early Canadian technology success story called AES Data in Montreal, when one more corporate re-organisation placed him under an ambitious new manager who decided to sacrifice a few good soldiers in his battle to cut costs and enhance his own performance in the eyes of senior executives. Dale had been a bad choice for the firing line. He had a history of hard work and delivering results and he had lots of strong supporters in the company who were upset that he had been shown the exit so abruptly.

Dale was shocked and angry and decided to fight back. He hired a lawyer who threatened to sue the company for wrongful dismissal. AES was quick to recognize their error and agreed to pay severance of two full year's salary. It was a turning point for Dale to leave the corporate world after the years of his increasing cynicism and disgust with the never-ending corporate politics and people pushing their own career plans over the needs of their employees and customers.

The cash settlement was a helpful start in finally going into business for himself.

Dale's wife, Susan, had been nervous about the sudden lack of security for their young family and the impact on the plans to send their kids to expensive private schools. Their son, Sean, was only ten and daughter, Keira, was eight. Susan was supportive of Dale's new business initiative, however, and joined him in pursuing the opportunities they saw in the fascinating new world of personal computers.

She willingly agreed to help at the office for the first year and Dale discovered she had an eye for design and marketing that were invaluable to the business. She managed to work a few hours a day at the office around the kids' schedules at elementary school and their extra-curricular activities. When the business could afford to replace her with a full-time employee, Dale hired Marie de Carlo and Susan dedicated herself again to the family and her own interests. She was a fit and active young woman, who was serious about competitive tennis at the local club, but was also dedicated to volunteering several hours a week at the palliative care centre in their neighbourhood. She and Dale had been introduced to palliative care when Dale's father was in the late stages of Alzheimer's disease and they had learned its value for the comfort it offered to patients and the families with a loved one approaching the end of life.

In starting the business, Dale had relied on his prior knowledge and experience with computer products from his three years with AES Data. AES claimed to have invented word-processing with the proprietary hardware and software that they sold to document-heavy organisations in business and government around the world. By the early 1980s, AES Data had annual sales revenue exceeding two-hundred million dollars with over two thousand employees in Canada, the U.S. and Europe and three manufacturing facilities in Montreal and Toronto. Unfortunately, the company didn't survive the onslaught of the more versatile and less expensive personal computers built by Apple and IBM, that offered much more than word-processing. Sales for AES declined dramatically. The turmoil caused continual adjustments of corporate strategy and the organisation and eventually led to Dale's abrupt departure.

During his time at AES Data, he had established important business contacts, including two associates in Toronto in the computer business, Don Leeman and Doug Maxwell. Dale worked with them to assess the opportunities for his business and to evaluate the low-cost offshore manufacturers who could meet his performance and design specifications for computer monitors.

Don Leeman and Doug Maxwell were two experienced businessmen who worked tightly together as business partners. They looked like they could be twin brothers, two pudgy, middle-aged men with thick wavy brown hair, who were usually wearing white shirts and ties with their jackets off, sleeves rolled up and ties pulled loose. They had been associates for over two decades, first at Electrohome, a Canadian television and stereo manufacturer, then for the last five years as the owners of a business importing computer products.

Don and Doug were impressed with Dale and his plan to launch a line of computer monitors and decided to invest with him in the new business. The name 3D Computer Products came from the three initial partners, Dale, Don and Doug. They liked the sound of 3D and enjoyed the attention it got from its association with the high-technology sounding 'three-dimensional'. The explanation didn't matter, they thought, so long as people remembered the name. Like 3M, famous for Scotch tape and Post-it notes, who cared that it was originally the Minnesota Mining and Manufacturing Company?

To be successful with computer monitors, Dale and his new partners had to compete effectively with major brand names like IBM and Hewlett Packard, who were using computer monitors made for them by the established TV manufacturers in the U.S. or Japan, like Zenith, Motorola, Hitachi, Toshiba and Sony.

Dale had done his research on the few personal computer monitors available in the market, and the manufacturers that could deliver them, before he visited their factories in Korea and Taiwan in early 1984. After ten days there, evaluating their capabilities and negotiating prices, he contracted with two qualified low-cost suppliers for private-label computer monitors under his newly branded product line, called EXL. He selected one manufacturer in Korea and one in Taiwan, to ensure the security of a second source of supply and to generate competition between the two suppliers. To further entice them both to offer the lowest possible costs, he persuaded his two associates in Toronto to sell the EXL-branded product line there too, and increase their combined purchase volumes.

Dale was determined to be a successful distributor in the computer business by retaining control over his brand name and his product lines. It was an important strategic advantage over the typical distribution business that sold third-party brands and was entirely dependent on the suppliers for products, pricing and delivery. In addition, the distributors had continuous pressure from competitors with the same products, unless their suppliers agreed to provide exclusivity to them in a particular market sector or geographical region.

The strength of 3D Computers in growing the business quickly came not only from Dale's emphasis on providing reliable performance with low-cost products, but also his skill in building customer loyalty through determined sales effort, attentive customer service and competent technical support.

As soon as the first products were available from the two suppliers, Dale spent a week driving around Montreal testing his pitch and his pricing on local computer retailers with samples of the EXL computer monitors in the back of his Toyota Camry station wagon. He proved the sales potential immediately and decided to open for business with a small office and warehouse in a low-rent commercial strip off the highway near his home. 3D Computers was among the first few local distributors serving the rapidly growing demand for personal computers in homes, offices and schools all over the province of Quebec.

Sales revenue grew quickly and Dale was able to reassure Susan that the family finances were secure again.

With expanding sales, Dale quickly recognized that he needed more space and more staff. He moved the business to an industrial park that sprawled between the major highways leading from Dorval International Airport to downtown Montreal. It was a central location and 3D Computers leased a three-bay unit with offices facing the street, parking spaces in front and a high-ceilinged warehouse with loading dock access at the back. Dale looked out from his corner office across the street to another row of industrial units in brick and steel with painted aluminum siding and colorful display signs for QuickXpress Couriers, Steve's HVAC, SuperSports Warehouse and many similar businesses that stretched through the industrial park for several blocks in all directions.

Dale wondered if any of them had been held-up for protection money.

Dumb ass, he thought, *I've got a big 3D Computer Products sign above the front door. It's like advertising for crooks, 'Come on in, help yourself!'*

The computer industry had become a popular target for smash-and-grab and midnight break-ins, even hold-ups at gun point. Insurance companies were raising premiums and demanding installation of high security alarm systems with direct telephone connection to the nearest police station.

He wondered if there was insurance against the protection racket.

Professional insurance versus Jacques' version of insurance? Not bloody likely.

He was on his own with this problem.

***

After that first visit from Jacques, Dale went home distracted by the questions and concerns running through his mind. The arrival of gangsters demanding protection money was not something he had ever expected. He thought it was only a problem for bars and restaurants in the rougher neighborhoods of Montreal.

Dale lived in the upper middle-class suburban neighborhood of the West Island about fifteen minutes from his office. It was usually a welcome relief from the stress and fatigue of work to be at home with Susan and their kids, Sean and Keira. Dale took pleasure in relaxing with his family and the friendly neighbors with their young families. Friendly young families in modern two-story homes on well-maintained properties, it was a pleasant, comfortable neighborhood.

That evening Dale was not in the mood to enjoy it.

He pulled into his driveway, recently plowed clear of snow, and parked in front of the garage.

"Hi Jerry," he called out to the neighbour next door who was scraping the snow and ice off his front steps.

Dale continued with his head down into the house, where he was greeted at the entrance by his daughter, Keira.

"Hi Daddy."

He stepped into the hallway and gave her a quick hug.

"Hi honey."

He waved to his wife, Susan, in the kitchen and went on upstairs past Sean's room, where he was lying on the bed reading. Dale dropped his briefcase on the sofa beside his desk in the spare bedroom that he used as an office and slumped into the high-backed swivel chair.

He was thinking, *what should I say to Susan?*

They normally shared everything important in their lives and Susan still had an interest in his business, but this wasn't something she needed to worry about yet, he thought.

They had met at university and were married in their early twenties. Susan became pregnant soon after they moved to Montreal while Dale was doing his MBA. Tragically, their first child, Lorraine Marie, was born prematurely and had only survived for two difficult weeks. It was a traumatic life-changing experience and caused them to be extremely dedicated and protective of Sean and Keira.

That evening they talked about the kids and their school activities. Dale wasn't ready to explain the threats and the demands for protection money, or 'insurance' as they called it. He couldn't explain the arrival of this thug Jacques, even to himself, and it was too soon to know what he could do about it. Too soon to go to the police. Maybe he could make some kind of a deal and they'd just go away.

Then he wouldn't have to worry Susan about it at all.

He had a restless night.

3.

Dale came in to the office the next morning and tried not to expect Jacques every few minutes. There was no sign of him. It was a long day.

Business continued as usual, shuffling paperwork, employees in and out of the office, phone calls from customers with questions and complaints, faxes from suppliers and bills to pay. Dale took a break from his desk for a tour of the warehouse and service department to speak with his employees. It was his preferred way of keeping in touch with staff and he was always open to their questions or complaints. Today, he was not listening very well.

Mid-winter in Montreal meant that it was dark by five-thirty and there was still no sign of Jacques. Dale waited.

"Good night, Marie," he said as she looked back at Dale with concern. She was always the last to leave.

Marie de Carlo had assumed the role of den mother at 3D Computers after she had been hired to replace Susan as office manager during the first year. She had been referred by a family friend and was returning to work after her own kids had all left home for university. In spite of her stern, officious manner, she was a warm, compassionate woman who treated Dale and Susan and all the staff at 3D Computers as her extended family.

Dale was starting to think he was safe for another day and he went to turn out the lights in the warehouse and lock up for the night. As he came back into the office area, the front door opened and there was Jacques.

"Did you think I'd forget you?" he said.

Dale silently waved him in and locked the front door behind him. He turned and led the way back to his office. They settled into their chairs, Dale behind the desk and Jacques sitting in front with a big black boot crossed over one knee. He didn't look any more friendly than yesterday. Same grey suit and gold chains, same burgundy silk shirt.

Same shirt as yesterday? Dale thought, *why am I worrying if he's wearing a clean shirt?*

Jacques waited for Dale to respond to the proposition he had left him with.

"Look," Dale said, "there's no way in Hell I can pay you a thousand in cash every week. How can we make this go away?"

Jacques sat quietly and looked around Dale's office, lingering on the family pictures on his desk and the long leather fur-trimmed coat hanging behind the door.

"We're not going away," he said. "We know you're doing very well, Mr. Hunter. Sorry about the broken tail light on your sporty BMW by the way."

Leaning forward, he looked intently at Dale.

"We're going to make this easy for you. Just arrange the cash for us every week. You can even put it through the books as insurance, so it'll look perfectly legit." He leaned back in his chair. "We're professionals you know, not burglars doing a smash and grab in the night."

Dale started to wonder if that was actually how this started. There had been a late night break-in at 3D Computers about four months ago. The thieves had avoided all the alarm systems by coming in through the roof behind the infra-red motion detectors that were pointed only at the peripheral doors and windows. They had used an extension ladder to get onto the roof, then dropped another through the hole they had cut in the flat galvanized metal. Once inside, they had grabbed computers from the office and about eighty monitors and several boxes of high value video cards from the warehouse, then climbed out onto the roof and back to the ground. Their truck must have been loaded near the back door where they were hidden from the street until they left. The stolen goods had never been recovered and Dale had never heard of anyone being arrested.

Now he wondered if the crooks had accessed his office computer and learned enough about him and his business to decide they should come back and squeeze him for more. Maybe that's how these guys identified their prey for the protection racket.

It doesn't matter now, thought Dale. *They know what they want and they're prepared to get violent if necessary.*

Jacques was French-Canadian, but this scam smelt and felt like the work of the Italian gangsters of Montreal with their New York Mafia connections. Dale had read about them in the regularly featured articles on organized crime in the *Montreal Gazette* and the *Journal de Montréal* newspapers.

He could see no way out.

"How about one payment and we're done?"

"Nope," Jacques said, "I prefer regular cash. Just build it into your weekly routine to look after me."

Dale couldn't tolerate the threats to Susan and the kids. There was no use pretending to be a tough guy and having somebody get hurt.

"Alright, I really don't like this arrangement, but I'll try to make it work. Just be sure to keep your half of the bargain. No interruptions to my business and no more threats to my family."

"Of course," said Jacques, "You pay and we deliver. No problem, my friend."

You're not my friend, you bastard, just take the money and leave me alone, thought Dale.

He handed Jacques the envelope with the cash in it that he'd placed earlier in his desk drawer. He agreed to leave an envelope marked 'Guaranteed Insurance' with the cash in it every Tuesday morning at the reception desk with Marie.

It was not a problem for Dale to come up with a thousand a week. He was taking regular cash advances from the business for himself and he could add more to cover the cash he needed for Jacques. He could vary the amounts and the timing, so it wouldn't raise any questions at the bank. He knew banks didn't like to see too much cash coming and going.

I don't want to raise any red flags, he thought. *Jacques was pretty clear about not getting the police involved, so I'm not taking any chances.*

Dale was intrigued by their methods that seemed so business-like. He wondered how they decided on a thousand a week. These guys didn't have MBAs and they probably didn't do market research to check the going rate for protection. Did they just pick a number to see if it sticks?

Very entrepreneurial, Dale thought, *maybe I should be more receptive.*

Hell no, these guys are crooks using violence to get what they want. But why did I settle for a thousand a week? Maybe I should have negotiated harder. Maybe I should skip a payment or short change them one week, just to prove how hard it is to come up with the cash. Nope, probably a better idea just to play along and do as I'm told. No need to provoke something worse than what I'm already dealing with.

Dale tried to work with these new demands. He started to keep stockpiles of cash in a small safe at home and in a locked cabinet drawer in his office and took what he needed to put in the envelope each week. It occurred to him that he was essentially being held hostage by this guy named Jacques and paying his own ransom in weekly installments. He wondered if he was committing a crime by paying for protection, then making it worse by money-laundering on top of it.

Too many questions went unanswered.

And now it was time to explain to Susan.

***

That evening after the kids had gone to bed, Dale and Susan were comfortably settled in the family room watching the ten o'clock National News on TV. Dale was stretched out in the armchair with his stocking feet on the coffee table and wearing his standard winter wardrobe of brown cords with a blue button-down shirt over a white tee shirt. Susan was stretched out beside him in her red-and-grey tracksuit from an afternoon at the tennis club, her blonde hair still tied back in a ponytail.

Dale sat up, reached for the remote control and turned the TV off.

Susan looked at him in surprise.

"Hey," she said, smiling, "why'd you do that?"

"Well, uh, I think we need to talk. There are some issues at work I think you should know about."

She sat back.

"Oh really, now what?"

"I think I need a scotch first."

"Oh? The business is finally driving you to drink?"

"Don't worry," said Dale, "Just one to help me relax. No need to remind me of the old party days at UBC, I'm never doing that again."

Susan smiled, but Dale was still embarrassed by the memories.

They had met at the University of British Columbia in Vancouver. While adjusting to the big city and the challenges of university, they had also tried the hard-partying student lifestyle. Dale wasn't at all experienced at heavy drinking and on one of their first dates he drank too much, got sick and passed out. It was a scary experience, as they both knew of drunken students who had died after passing out and choking to death on their own vomit. After that incident, Dale never again lost his self-control to alcohol.

Susan was very supportive and understanding of the business demands on Dale, but she wasn't driven by the same entrepreneurial ambition. They both came from small-town British Columbia, but Susan was an only child raised by laid-back American draft-dodging hippy parents. They weren't at all impressed by Dale's hard-won business success and he had given up trying. He was satisfied with their keen interest in Susan and the kids.

Dale got up and went to the tall sideboard where the liquor was stored behind a closed door on the top shelf. He took down a crystal glass and splashed some Johnny Walker Red Label into it, no water, no ice.

"Do you want something?"

"Not now," Susan said, watching him closely, "Just tell me what's going on."

"OK," Dale said, as he sat back down. "Here's what's going on." He took a sip of the scotch.

"As you know, we've always had a few people around us who play outside the rules. Even outside the law sometimes, but we usually avoid getting drawn into it ourselves. Unfortunately, some very bad people have now come after us, too."

Susan sat still as he took another sip.

"Today I had to make a deal with the criminals myself."

She tried to remain calm, but gradually became more alarmed as Dale described the arrival of Jacques and the demand for a thousand dollars in cash every week. He mentioned the smashed tail light, since Susan would see it anyway and he didn't want to start lying to her, but he was vague about the threats to the family.

I'll worry about that enough for both of us for now, he thought.

When he was finished, Susan glanced down the hall, thinking of the kids upstairs in bed.

"Jesus, Dale," she said quietly, "we have to call the cops. Right now, before this goes any further."

Dale shook his head.

"No, not now, not yet. It's too risky and this guy's already shown me he's capable of violence, so I don't want to provoke him at all. Let me look after it. I'll see what I can do to end it. In the meantime, we can manage the thousand dollars a week."

Susan was shaking her head, but she said no more.

She knew Dale well enough to know he had made up his mind and was determined to look after it on his own.

4.

Dale loved running his own business, at least until all this started. This was his first encounter with the real gangsters in Montreal. The risk of violent crime threatening his business and his family was unfamiliar territory.

He had always been ambitious and competitive. He loved to win and he hated cheaters. He resented that playing by the rules always seemed to make it harder. He knew some of his competitors broke the law, ignored government regulations and taxes and did cash under the table. Dale was proud to be winning most of his battles with those competitors. And he was still playing by the rules.

Up until Jacques arrived, Dale was enjoying his success. It had been worth taking a chance and betting on his own business. He had stubbornly refused to return to the corporate world after losing his job at AES and declined similar offers worth over $80,000 a year. Not everyone thought he had made good decisions turning them all down. Some friends and relatives, Susan's parents in particular, had warned him not to let go of the security and the income from a steady job.

"No way you'll ever do that well in your own business."

They were wrong.

Sales had gone from zero to a hundred thousand a month in just six months and he was now regularly doing over a million a month and paying himself accordingly. He had definitely found the formula, even if he couldn't explain it. He kept it simple.

"Just 'Sell like Hell, all the time,'" he constantly reminded his staff. "We're a small company and everyone has to think sales. Sales, sales and more sales." He knew he was getting through to them when even the receptionist and the shipper were bringing him sales opportunities.

The new business in Montreal grew fast under Dale's leadership. But rapid growth meant that Dale's partners were getting uncomfortable with the level of borrowing that was required. The bank was also getting anxious about the high debt load and 'over-trading,' meaning they thought Dale was selling more than he could finance. They were all nervous passengers who wanted to get off the risky ride that Dale found so exciting.

Dale did not accept their concerns. He saw rapid growth as a sign of success. How could selling too much ever be a problem? Increasing sales solved the problems, he thought.

"Nothing succeeds like success," his Dad used to tell him and he believed it. He discovered that the better he did, the more people wanted to do business with him. But the bank and his partners balked at providing the additional financing he needed to continue at his rapid pace. A new deal had to be made.

So Dale decided he had to buy out his partners in the business and continue without them. That meant assuming additional risk himself by pledging his house to the bank and cashing out the savings that were intended to fund his future retirement. Retirement would have to wait.

Susan had to be persuaded that it was a risk worth taking, but she eventually agreed to join Dale in his ambitious plans. She knew she would always be his most important partner in life and business and no agreements needed to be signed to prove it.

Once Dale had added to his personal investment in the business, the bank provided sufficient additional financing to allow him to buy out his partners' initial investment.

Don Leeman and Doug Maxwell quickly accepted Dale's offer to pay them three times their original investment of $50,000 over the next two years. They remained as partners in the sale and distribution of EXL products in Canada and Dale provided ongoing access to the monitor product line at a very low mark-up over his costs from the manufacturers. They maintained a good working relationship and occasionally shared other product lines that were complementary to their independent businesses.

After Dale's financing constraints were relieved and the new partnership arrangements concluded, he was able to dedicate his efforts again to accelerating growth and improving profits.

Making money alone was never that important to Dale. He hadn't grown up poor. His parents both had good jobs and the family had never had to struggle to make ends meet. Dale had always done well financially, in corporate jobs and in consulting after his MBA. Now he was doing better than ever. He loved what it meant for him and his family, spending without hesitation or concern about budget limits. Kids in private school, holiday cruises and expensive resort vacations. He looked after himself well too, with smart, fashionable clothes and a new sports car, all in keeping with the youthful, energetic image that he wanted to project.

He did admit that driving a BMW M3 sports coupe was good for his ego as well as a satisfying reward for the long hours of hard work and the stressful financial risks he had taken. It had been a special pleasure to walk into the dealership and pay for the car with a personal check of $42,000.

He had learned not to boast about it though, after his customer, Alex Simpson, had reacted.

"Jesus, I knew I was paying you too much for those damn EXL monitors."

After that Dale tried to be more discreet, but he was keeping the car.

His conspicuous success had its downside. Jealous competitors tried hard to steal his customers. His sales reps occasionally argued they weren't getting enough credit for helping him make all that money and suggested they should be compensated more in line with their contribution, as they called it. Some of his biggest customers persuaded themselves that they were essential to his success and they too asked for special consideration. Dale needed them all to work with him to sustain his rapid business growth, so he responded with his own creative approaches and sometimes sweetened the pot to keep everyone hungry for more, but always within what he called 'reasonable limits'.

The thousand dollars a week for protection fit within those reasonable limits for Dale. It was not much of a burden to his cash flow and he was prepared to ignore the fact that he was now doing business with criminals. He could accept the minor annoyance.

Unfortunately, it didn't remain a minor annoyance.

***

Dale had handed Jacques the first envelope of cash himself. The next week a local courier service arrived for the envelope that had been left with Marie de Carlo in a locked drawer at the reception desk.

It was the third Tuesday when Marie looked out the window beside her desk as a loud Harley Davidson pulled up to the curb beside the front door. It was unusual to see a motorcycle on the streets of

Montreal in February, but it had been mild and warm enough that the roads were bare and dry. The salt and sand-covered snow banks were still piled along the edges of the streets and parking lots and would remain there until March.

The leather-clad biker strolled into reception and without removing his helmet or lifting the black visor, spoke in a muffled voice.

"Pick up for Guaranteed Insurance."

Marie looked warily into the black visor at a reflection of the office around her. The biker stood in front of her as she unlocked the drawer and placed the envelope on the counter top at the front of her reception desk.

The biker then pulled out a folded note from his inside jacket pocket and put it on top of the envelope. The muffled voice spoke again.

"For Mr. Hunter."

Marie paused to look at the envelope with the note lying on top of it. Then she picked them up and went down the hall to put both on Dale's desk. He turned from his keyboard and screen to look up at her, then at the note placed with the envelope.

"There's a biker here to pick up the Guaranteed Insurance envelope. He gave it back to me with this note for you," said Marie.

She went back to her desk to keep an eye on the biker.

Dale frowned and reached for the note. He unfolded it and read the scrawled handwriting.

> Maintenant c'est $2000 par semaine.
>
> Ajouter $1000 aujourd'hui.
>
> Jacques

It was not welcome news. Jacques now wanted two thousand a week with a thousand added to the envelope today. Apparently the payments for 'insurance' were going up and the increase was not open to negotiation. Jacques hadn't even appeared in person to make the demand.

Dale took a long breath and considered his options. It was getting expensive, but at least there were no new threats. He turned to unlock the top right drawer of the cabinet behind his desk and lifted up the tray of pens and pencils to take a wad of hundred-dollar bills out from under it. He counted out a thousand dollars to put in the envelope, then locked the drawer again. He tossed the note in his waste basket and took the envelope back to Marie. He dropped it on her desk without looking at the biker and returned to his office.

Just one more challenge, he thought.

Among all the hungry vultures picking away for pieces of him, he now had a snarling jackal named Jacques leaping into the fray to take a bite. The bites were getting bigger, but Dale was never going to let his business collapse into a lifeless carcass.

***

After another three weeks of business as usual and no more surprises, Dale was getting comfortable again with his arrangement until, suddenly, Jacques himself walked into the offices of 3D Computers.

It was another Tuesday morning and he asked Marie for the Guaranteed Insurance envelope. She remembered him from his first disturbing visit, before this strange process started. She unlocked the drawer and handed him the envelope. He immediately walked down the hall to Dale's office, without asking permission.

Dale looked up from his desk to see Jacques standing in the doorway.

"Hello Hunter, glad to see your car got fixed OK. Looks good. I hear business is good too. I thought I should drop in and see if I can help you do even better."

Dale said nothing.

Jacques stepped into Dale's office and plopped his ass into the chair in front of Dale's desk. He got comfortable, then continued.

"Now that we're business partners, I think I should send some more customers your way. You know I can be very persuasive."

He leaned back and looked around the office.

"More customers will be good for sales and it'll help you pay the premium increase to three thousand next week. Maybe you can even recommend me some new customers to pay insurance."

Dale was quick to reply.

"Hell no! Stay away from my customers. I don't need anybody knowing I'm working with gangsters. Goddammit! Three thousand is too much. I can't handle that every week!"

Jacques shrugged his shoulders and got up from his chair. He turned to the door, then looked back at Dale.

"We'll see. You need to get sales up, man. Insurance is expensive. And I know you want the protection for your wife and kids. See you soon."

That's when Dale decided this had to end.

He couldn't continue to pull cash out of thin air and they were never going to leave him and his family alone. The demands and the threats were clearly going to get worse. Apparently they had no problem with squeezing the golden goose until they killed it and he didn't want that to be the unhappy ending to this fairy tale.

He needed to gain control and figure out how to end it somehow.

He thought again about getting the cops involved and making the call he had been warned not to make. He had to find a way that didn't cause him new problems. And didn't put his family more at risk.

5.

The morning after Jacques' visit, Dale took a different route past Dorval Airport and turned away from 3D Computers to go down Cote-de-Liesse, the two-mile stretch of highway from the airport to the Decarie Expressway that was lined with hotels and commercial buildings along the service roads.

He pulled in to park at an aluminum clad glassed-in eight-story building on the south service road and went up to the third floor. He walked down the hall and buzzed at the door of *Phoenix systèmes de bureau*. The painted lettering on the reinforced glass window beside the entrance showed that the company did computer consulting and installation of office networks. The door clicked to unlock it and he went inside to a large office that had the solid professional look of a legal or accounting firm.

This wasn't one of Dale's typical retail customers in a trashy storefront run by a young computer techie using the only sales technique he knew, boasting "Lowest Prices!" and selling hard to unsophisticated buyers of home computers. Jean-Guy Brassard was the owner of Phoenix Office Systems and was an engineer with an MBA like Dale, who sold more complex computer systems and software applications to knowledgeable, demanding corporate and government buyers.

Dale hadn't called ahead for an appointment, so he explained to the receptionist that he just wanted to speak to Jean-Guy briefly.

When he came out to the front desk, Dale asked his friend and customer if he could borrow their small conference room after lunch for a private teleconference.

"Just for half an hour or so."

"Sure, Dale, *pas de problème,*" Jean-Guy said, "You're welcome here anytime."

He paused, but Dale said, "Thanks," and quickly exited before Jean-Guy could ask the questions that were on his mind.

When Dale came back to Phoenix about one-thirty in the afternoon, he looked in on Jean-Guy.

"*Merci, Jean-Guy, ça ne sera pas long,* I won't be long."

Jean-Guy looked up from the paperwork on his desk, "*Bonjour, Dale.*" Then he scowled and continued, "*Mais c'est très mystérieux, ton affaire. J'espère que tu ne fais pas des choses illégales de mon bureau.*"

"No, no, no. Not very mysterious and never illegal," Dale laughed. "Not really my style, you know."

The scowl disappeared and Jean-Guy laughed too. "*Ah oui, c'est vrai.* It's true. You are one of the few honest men left in this business. That's why we do business with you. It's definitely not the product or the price."

"Whatever works," said Dale. "Glad to know I can still fool some of the people some of the time."

He stepped into Jean-Guy's office and sat down in front of him.

"So, do you have a big order for me?" Dale asked.

Jean-Guy Brassard was slim with neatly-trimmed dark hair and moustache, sitting at his executive desk in a sharply pressed white shirt and bright blue tie. His grey pin-stripe suit jacket was hung on the back of the armchair beside the conference table in the corner. He leaned forward and folded his hands together on the desk.

"*Pas encore, mon ami*, not yet. But it's government year-end soon and all the department heads in Quebec City and Ottawa are trying hard to spend their budgets before March thirty-first. I have several big quotes outstanding and should get some decisions this week. I hope you have lots of stock."

"We do. Ready to do even better than last year. So good luck with those quotes. We want the business too."

"Your EXL monitors are included Dale, don't worry. Lots of business coming your way, *c'est certain*."

"OK, sounds good."

With a quick thumbs-up, Dale got up and went down the hall from Jean-Guy's office and into the small conference room.

He closed the door and pulled out his notebook for the phone number he had written in it the day before. He knew he was risking repercussions, but he had decided to call the cop he knew from the break-in at his warehouse last year.

Detective Pierre Forsey had investigated and he had impressed Dale as calm and competent, no bullshit and no drama. Forsey, a veteran of the Montreal Urban Community police force working out of Station 21 downtown, had seen it all before and was wise to the criminal elements of Montreal and their long history with the Mafia and biker-gangs. He knew the thugs were now finding easy money in high value computer products. Computer stores and distribution warehouses like Dale's were struggling to maintain adequate security measures and to pay the high insurance premiums to keep ahead of the criminals.

Dale reached Forsey on the second call to the station and reminded him of their meeting after the break-in. Forsey remembered him.

"How're you doing? I hope your insurance got settled all right."

"Yeah, but they didn't make it easy," said Dale. "They spent a long time making sure it wasn't an inside job and even suggested maybe I had arranged it, just for the insurance."

"That happens," said Forsey, "some businesses are looking for the easy money. Hope they were satisfied that wasn't the case for you."

"Yeah, they eventually paid out on the $180,000 worth of product that was stolen. But I hate to think what my premiums will be next year."

Dale hesitated. He was having second thoughts on introducing Forsey to the situation. He had to take the threats to his family seriously.

Forsey heard the long silence.

"You don't have a new problem, do you?"

Dale took a deep breath and exhaled loudly enough for Forsey to know more was coming. It was time to get on with it.

"Well ..., yes, actually I do. This time I'm in deep shit with some very dangerous people. They've already threatened me and my family, if I even talk to you. So we have to be very careful."

"I see," said Pierre, then before Dale could explain any further, "Sounds like you're getting hit for protection money."

Strangely relieved, Dale relaxed into his chair.

"OK, you know what I'm talking about. Now how do we stop it without me getting hurt by these guys?"

Now Forsey was quiet for a few seconds.

"Well, you're right, these are dangerous people and they can be hard for us to get at. Tell me the whole story."

After listening to Dale unload and tell him about Jacques and the original demand for one thousand a week, then two and now three thousand, with more threats to his family, Forsey replied.

"You do have a problem."

"Thanks, I knew that already."

"Well look, we could start surveillance and pick up Jacques at some point, but we probably won't get him to tell us who he's working for and they might still take it out on you, if they find out we're onto them."

"You're not helping me here."

Another long pause from Forsey before he spoke.

"Listen, we don't want to add to your troubles, unless we can be sure to end it for you. Sometimes they learn pretty quickly that we've been contacted and then things can get rough for you. We know the guys working in your area, but they also know we're watching them. It's kind of a delicate dance, until we can get enough on them to make an arrest. Even then we'd like to be sure we're getting the right guys, because if we don't stop it at the top, then they just replace their man on collections with another guy."

Dale shifted in his chair. He dropped his pen on the pad in front of him and put his head in his hand, as Forsey continued.

"I'm going to suggest we try another route. I think we should fight these bad guys with another bad guy, for now anyway. Somebody who can beat them at their own game and who can be more creative than us. And he can't be tied to you."

Dale sat up.

"How does that work?"

"I'll have a guy named Frank call you, Frank the Fixer."

"Jesus, this is really starting to sound crazy. You're suggesting my solution is to add another bad guy to this nightmare. A guy called Frank the Fixer?"

"Listen, he will find a way to make them go away and he'll make sure they never know you had anything to do with it. I work with him a lot. He's on our side, but he plays by his own rules, if necessary. Let's arrange for you to talk to Frank and satisfy yourself. I'll see what I can do from this end. Believe me, you're not alone. We know about these guys and we're trying to shut them down."

Dale pushed his papers back into the file folder on the table, squaring them up neatly.

"OK, I'll talk to him. It sounds risky, but I don't have a better idea. This has to stop before they kill my business. And I don't want them coming after me or my family. Have your guy call me, but not at the office. He can ask for me at this number." He gave Forsey the phone number for Phoenix Systems. "I think this line is more secure than mine, but I'll be getting a car phone soon, so maybe we can use that when it's installed and I figure out how to use it. I'll be here again tomorrow, let's say two o'clock."

"OK, let's do that. I'll give Frank your story and you can give him the go ahead. Bye for now."

Dale put the phone down and looked at the closed door of the conference room. He was aware of the sweat beading on his forehead and he wiped it away with his forearm. This was not something he wanted to explain to Jean-Guy or anybody else. Now he was working with the cops and they were sending him to somebody called Frank the Fixer.

He leaned back in the chair.

What the hell is happening here? Why me? I could be back home in beautiful BC drinking a cold beer with my feet up looking out at the Rockies.

Dale loved that spectacular view of jagged peaks thrust above the tree line that defined the border with Alberta where the Rockies stretched across the horizon above the Kootenay River near his old home town. The bright lights and historic sites of Montreal were impressive, but never that spectacular.

So why the hell am I here making myself miserable trying to run a business that's under attack by criminals?

Dale had grown up in the small town of Cranbrook, in the southeast corner of British Columbia, Canada's western-most province. His father was a pipe-fitter at the local pulp mill and his mother was an elementary school teacher. His younger brother and sister both had young families now too and still lived in Cranbrook.

Dale had always been the annoying older brother, well-behaved, top of the honor roll, President of the Student's Council, captain of the hockey team. A popular kid, but a loner. Thinking a lot and worrying about his future. His grade-eight English teacher had reassured him.

"You bright kids always worry too much. You'll be just fine."

He had continued to worry and spend too much time alone inside his head.

Dale's arrival at UBC in Vancouver was a big awakening. He was dazzled by his first exposure to the big city and suddenly discovered he wasn't the brightest kid in class or the top recruit for the UBC Thunderbirds hockey team. It rattled his confidence. But he buckled down and gradually recovered his self-assurance. First he made the hockey team. Then he succeeded in getting far better marks on the Christmas exams than any of his old classmates from high school. He learned that talent and hard work still made a difference.

He even came out of his shell at UBC and joined in the frequent social events for engineering students designed to give them a break from their onerous study schedule and to introduce them to some girls. There were none in his engineering classes. During the second year, he met and fell in love with his future wife, Susan Bowness, a nursing student.

A few years studying engineering convinced Dale that he had zero mechanical aptitude and even less interest in things mechanical. He discovered instead that he was attracted to the mysteries of the business world. Economics and finance were more appealing than engineering, so he took as many courses as he could fit in. He did well in all of them, while working hard to avoid letting his engineering marks slide downhill.

After graduation he accepted a job with a small manufacturer of industrial steel cabinets, so that he could enjoy city life in Vancouver with Susan and start making some money. But within a year he had struggled enough with the engineering and he began looking for an MBA School to change the direction of his career. He was soon offered a scholarship to go to McGill University in Montreal, the heart of French Canada. The scholarship and the attraction of Montreal made it easy to decide. Susan insisted, however, that he marry her before she would agree to come with him. It was arranged for that summer in her hometown of Nelson, a popular hippie hangout in the mountains of central British Columbia.

Dale had been introduced to the city of Montreal and the province of Québec during a summer vacation trip to Expo '67 on his way to Europe for a month of hitchhiking. It was his first experience with bilingual Canada and it proved that his high school French was almost entirely useless, but he still found the historic, multi-cultural city fascinating.

Montreal was founded in the early 1600s by French colonists and fur traders and strategically located on a large island about thirty miles long by ten miles wide in the broad Saint Lawrence River below the white water rapids that made portages necessary to continue on the waterways westward. Transportation routes were later improved by construction of the Lachine Canal in the 1850s and the Saint Lawrence Seaway in the 1960s.

Montreal remained at the heart of Canadian industry, economic development and political intrigue for over three hundred years. In the 1960s, major political reforms began with the Quiet Revolution as the provincial government addressed long-standing discontent with the English dominance that had existed since the British conquest of Quebec in 1759. Continuing agitation led to the more radical separatist movement and election of the *Parti Québécois* in 1976 whose strong anti-English and anti-establishment politics and threats to pull the province out of Canada caused a severe decline in economic prosperity for the city and the province with an exodus of English talent and capital down Highway 401 to Toronto.

Dale knew all these negatives of living and working as an Anglo in the province of Quebec, so why had he stayed through all that turmoil? He loved Montreal for its history, its bilingualism, the French culture, vibrant life style and relaxed friendliness that appealed to small-town people like him. He preferred Montreal over the status-conscious snobs of Toronto who, he thought, were always trying too hard to be as posh and sophisticated as New York, London or Los Angeles.

After his MBA at McGill, Dale remained with his young family in Montreal and looked for a good job to recover from two years as a full-time student draining the bank account. Typical of MBAs at the time, especially those with prior engineering degrees, he was hired by a consulting firm, called TS&K. After five years there working as a management consultant with a variety of business clients, he was recruited by AES Data to join their ambitious young management team. It was an exciting and challenging time to be in the rapidly evolving new world of micro-computers. He expected to build a career at AES until the sudden decline of the business and their decision to force him out. Through all of the career moves and now running his own business, Dale still loved Montreal as a place to live and raise his family.

Now if he could just get rid of these new obstacles and get back to making money and enjoying life.

6.

After the conversation with Detective Pierre Forsey, Dale went back to his office wondering, *who the hell is Frank the Fixer? What can he do that the cops can't?*

Dale worried again that he had made a mistake getting Forsey involved. But now the wheels were in motion and he'd have to deal with the consequences, whatever happened.

The next afternoon before two, Dale was back at Phoenix Systems and waiting in the same conference room. He spread out some files onto the conference table. His mind wandered around the situation and the players involved, until the receptionist buzzed him on the intercom.

"Somebody named Frank is on line three for you, Mr. Hunter."

He picked up the line.

"Hello Frank, this is Dale, thanks for calling."

"Mm-hmm," was all he heard.

Dale continued.

"I assume Detective Forsey told you my story. He says you might be able to help with my problem."

"Maybe."

That didn't sound encouraging.

"Do you have a last name, by the way?"

"Not for now." Followed by silence.

"OK."

This is not going well, thought Dale.

"Yeah, Forsey told me your story," Frank continued. "Apparently there's a guy named Jacques, I need to take care of for you."

"Right, a big nasty French-Canadian sonofabitch. He drives a red Dodge Ram pick-up, if that helps. I hope you can take care of him. He's already costing me too much with this protection racket and now he wants more. It has to stop. What can you do about it? Forsey says you can do more than he can."

"I'll find a way, don't worry."

"Don't tell me not to worry. This guy has threatened me and my family if I talk to anybody, so I'm already worrying. I need to know what you're going to do about it. How do I reach you when I need to?"

"You don't. I'll reach you if I need you and I don't need you for now," said Frank.

Dale sat back, shaking his head listening to Frank. His accent was not French-Canadian and English was clearly not his first language.

"Forsey gave me enough to work with and he's looking after my fee. Just keep doing business as usual with Jacques. He'll never know what hit him or where I came from, but he'll leave you alone soon enough. You'll hear from me in a week or so."

This was sounding more positive and Dale had no choice, anyway. He wasn't being asked for more cash, but he was not optimistic his problem was going to get solved any time soon.

"OK, call me in my car, not the office, when you have something for me. I had a car phone installed this morning and it should be more secure from Jacques and his friends, so let's see if we can make that work."

He gave Frank his mobile phone number. Dale wasn't that pleased with the ugly car phone that had been installed in his sleek and sporty BMW coupe. The bulky handset was attached to the centre console beside the stick shift with wires tucked into the upholstery and running to a mic clipped to his sun visor and through the rear panel into the trunk where a heavy square battery was fastened beside the six-pack CD player that he had installed a few months earlier. The car phone was only useful as a mobile office phone and neither removable, nor portable. The installer had assured him the technology would quickly get lighter, smaller, more portable and a lot less expensive than the $2800 that Dale had paid for it.

"I'm usually on the road to work between seven-thirty and eight," he said to Frank. "You can call me then. I don't want to see you at the office and I'll count on you to keep me and my family out of this."

"Understood."

Frank hung up.

***

On a cold grey winter afternoon a few days after Dale's conversation with Frank the Fixer, a black Cadillac Seville rolled down Sainte Catherine Street not far from Montreal Police Station No. 21 and stopped near the corner of Peel Street below a large neon sign that read, *Peel Pub, Bien manger, bien vivre! Eat well, Live well!*

The Caddy backed into an open parking space. The driver's door opened and a tall, well-dressed young black man got out, walked to the entrance of the Pub and went inside.

He looked around and then went to sit with a sour-faced older man at a well-worn table against the wall near the back of the Pub. A waiter came to their table and took their orders, a club sandwich and a smoked meat plate with two draft beers, one Molson Ex, one Alexander Keith.

They made an odd pair. Frank the Fixer was a good-looking, hard-muscled young African in a chic brown leather jacket, tight-fitting navy turtle-neck and blue jeans sitting tall across from a slouching Detective Pierre Forsey in a wrinkled brown wool suit with his slush and salt-splattered grey felt topcoat draped over the empty chair beside them.

"You're telling me that Jacques Talbot isn't working for Gino Boncanno on this one?" Frank said, after the waiter left their table.

"That's right. When I spoke to Gino, he didn't know what I was talking about."

"He would have backed off otherwise?"

Forsey scratched his scalp and the reddish-grey curls moved around the large fleshy ears that looked like giant malformed moths stuck in the tangles at the side of his head.

"Maybe. Sometimes if the mark comes to us, Gino agrees to shut it down to help us look good and keep it under the radar for him." He scratched again.

"Sometimes we agree to let him scare the poor bastard into calling us off. And Gino is very generous if we make that arrangement." He grinned, "Whatever happens, he decides. But he wasn't happy to hear about Jacques doing some moonlighting this time."

"I guess he's trying to do a little better for himself." Frank smiled. "Like the rest of us, eh Pierre? You seem to be doing alright working for both sides. But how do you explain it to the top dogs at the cop shop?"

"Don't worry about me, Frank. They're all too fucking stupid and useless to catch the crooks, so they're never going to catch up with me, either. Anyway, I deserve better after more than twenty years putting up with all their shit. Half the top dogs are on the take, so why shouldn't I make a little on the side too?"

"Sounds complicated with bosses on both sides," Frank said. "Maybe you can manage it, Pierre, but it's not for me. I like to make my own decisions. With no bosses checking up on me. I just do whatever works. Sometimes Somalian style, sometimes *Québécois*."

Pierre looked thoughtful, took another bite of smoked meat and wiped the yellow streak of mustard off his cheek with the paper napkin.

Frank continued.

"So what do you want me to do on this one?"

"You're not working for me or this guy Hunter now Frank, you're working for Gino. And he wants to send a message that working for him is a full-time, one hundred per cent exclusive arrangement. No more side deals. He's really pissed that Jacques was using him for leverage to scare this guy Hunter."

"OK, I'll take care of it. Does he want him dead?"

"Dead's not necessary, as long as he gets the message. Probably better if he lives to tell the tale." Forsey chuckled.

"OK," Frank shrugged. "Does Gino know he'll owe me?"

"Oh, yeah. He'll pay more than I do. Just let me know how much you want when the work is done."

"You can tell him ten grand is good and I'll let you know when it's done. Give me a few days."

They dug into their lunch and the talk turned to hockey. They agreed the Canadiens were having a good season and should make the playoffs in the spring.

***

"Hi Daddy, are you coming to my ringette game?"

Dale's blonde daughter, Kiera, in a pale green ski jacket and dark blue track pants, bounced into Dale's office ahead of her mother and plopped a bag lunch on his desk.

Dale came around the desk and gave her a big hug.

"Hi sweetheart, I'll try to get there later, but you have a good game, OK? Score one for me, I know you can do it."

Dale was not a big fan of ringette, which he saw as a pale imitation of hockey, invented just for girls. He thought it was like cheating to use a straight stick thrust into a rubber ring compared to the skill required for stickhandling with a hockey puck. But Kiera loved it more than figure skating and Sean's minor hockey wasn't much more entertaining anyway.

Dale tried to show an interest and support his kids in all their sports and extra-curricular activities, but he was often too busy to attend their events after school and relied on Susan to keep track of their schedules and remind him where and when he should show up.

"Daddy's busy, sweetheart," she said, "He has to work late, but I'm sure he'll see you before bedtime."

She turned to Dale.

"If you're going to put pressure on the poor girl, you could come to her games a little more often and show some support."

Dale looked at her.

"I've got a lot going on, you know, and it's not all business."

"I know Dale, the stress is showing on you. But a break with the kids once in a while would be good for you, too."

"You're right. I'll try to get there today, soon as I'm done here."

"It's alright. I'm not trying to put pressure on you, either. But it's a school night, if you don't make it to the game, try to be home by eight o'clock."

Sean, still in his school uniform with the crest on the blazer pocket and his white shirt-tail hanging out of grey pants, had been tagging along behind. Two years older, he was quieter and more serious than his sister. He had come slowly down the hall, checking out each person along the way with a polite "Hello," peering curiously at what they were doing. He was interested in everything that was going on, the telephones ringing, the scrolling computer screens and people hustling between offices sharing paperwork and chatting. He usually made a detour into the warehouse to check on the boxes coming and going from the piles stacked high to the ceiling and covering most of the floor area. He was fascinated by the service department, where the technicians fiddled with tools inserted into the open electronics on the bench. He watched there for a minute, then wandered on into Dale's office.

"Hi Dad, how's business?"

A future entrepreneur, thought Dale, *I'll have to get him in here as soon as he's old enough to help. Maybe he'll run this place someday.*

"Business is good, Sean. Lots of work to do and we should have a desk free for you here pretty soon." He put an arm around his son's shoulders and pulled him close. "You think you could help us make a few more sales? We have lots of stock to move in the back."

"I don't want to be in sales, Dad," said Sean looking up with disgust, "I want to work on computers. Sales is boring."

"OK," Dale laughed, "but you better do well at school in math and science, if you want to work on computers."

He rubbed Sean's head and ushered them all back out of his office. "I'll see you guys, later. Where's Kiera's game?" he asked Susan.

"At Pointe Claire Arena near the school," she said. "The game starts at six."

"OK," said Dale. "Thanks for the late lunch. I'll finish up here in a bit and see you there."

He held the door for them as they went back out to the station wagon and called out, "Go, Keira, go!" She giggled and climbed into the back seat beside Sean.

Susan looked back at him shaking her head and blew a kiss before she got the kids settled and buckled in.

Man, I'm a lucky guy, thought Dale. *Now how do I keep my beautiful family safe from creeps like Jacques and his friends?*

***

He had just settled back in his office to tidy up before leaving for the ringette game, when there was another interruption.

"Dale, can I see you a minute?"

It was Richard Séguin in the doorway. At forty-three, Richard was the oldest technician in the service department. Not the best technician, but hard-working, responsible and ambitious. He had taken the initiative to put himself through technical college after getting laid off from a furniture manufacturer in the Eastern Townships. He was the first technician hired by Dale to help with technical support and product repairs.

"*Mais oui, Richard, comment ça va?* What's up?"

Richard was well over six feet tall and two hundred pounds with big hands that didn't fit easily around the tools and into the tight spaces inside a monitor case. He had a smooth-shaved bald head and a drooping 1970s era mustache that usually looked incongruous around his big smile. Today, it fit well with his sombre expression.

He sat down uneasily in front of Dale.

"I have some news and I don't think you're gonna be happy about it."

Dale waited for more.

"Yeah, I've decided to leave for another job. I got an offer from *InfoCité* last week and I told them today I would take it."

"Jesus, Richard, you want to work for André Lebeau?"

Dale knew *InfoCité* and the owner, André Lebeau, as an occasional customer. He was not one of Dale's favorite customers, always pushing for special deals and selling at prices that were too low for him to be playing by the rules.

Apparently he has no qualms about raiding my staff either, thought Dale.

"I know he doesn't have a great reputation," said Richard, "but I kinda like him. He says he'll put me in sales and he's offering five hundred a week, plus commission, if I meet my sales quota. All cash, no taxes."

"Yeah, that sounds like André," said Dale. "But I've never trusted him, so be sure he delivers what he's offering you. You're at risk there, Richard. Be careful you don't get caught up in his breaking the law with cash under the table and avoiding taxes. He's probably dealing in stolen product too, so stay away from that stuff."

"We had a long conversation last time I was there and he tells me I'm too charming to be a technician." The smile was back.

"Too charming to be a good technician, that's for sure," said Dale. "Look Richard, we could try you in sales, but not at that price and I don't do cash, as you know." *At least, I didn't used to,* he thought.

"Yeah, I know. Sorry Dale, but I think it's time for a change for me."

"OK Richard, maybe this is a good opportunity for you. Just remember there's no coming back if it doesn't work out."

"Oh." Richard looked concerned and said, "I thought you would be here if I need to come back."

"Nope. In my experience anybody that comes back just does too much bitching about what they hated so much the first time. It poisons the water for everybody. If you leave, there's no coming back. It has to be a final decision."

He paused and watched Richard think it over.

"You sure you still want to leave?"

"Yeah, sorry Dale," Richard nodded. "It's really been a good experience here and I appreciate the chance you gave me to learn this business. But it's time for me to move on."

"OK, Richard, good luck." Dale stood to shake his hand. "Just tell Monique when you're leaving and she'll get your payroll finalized. I have to go to a ringette game."

As Richard left, Dale grabbed his EXL coffee mug and went down the hall for a fresh cup.

Just what I need, another headache, he thought.

3D Computer Products was already short of technicians and they were finding it difficult to keep up with the high rate of product returns for warranty repair.

He suddenly remembered the ringette game again. He drank his coffee quickly and rinsed the cup in the sink, then went back to his office, took his coat off the hook behind the door and headed for the rink.

***

Dale worried about Richard working at *InfoCité* with André Lebeau, as he remembered his most recent encounter there, about two weeks earlier.

He had been analyzing sales reports and planning for the next few months of deliveries from Korea and Taiwan. His desk and conference table were unusually disorganized with printouts spread everywhere.

One of the sales reps, Sylvie Cloutier, had knocked on the door and leaned in.

"Dale, I have André Lebeau from *InfoCité* on the line. He just placed an order for a hundred EXL-1439 monitors and it's over his credit limit. He won't do COD, but he said he'll pay you cash if you come by this evening. He wants the stock tomorrow."

The sonofabitch is just testing how much I'll bend over for him, Dale thought, *but it'll be about $37,000 and I could use the cash for Jacques.*

"OK, let's see. It's Thursday, so they'll be open 'til nine, tell him I'll come by the store about seven."

"Fine," said Sylvie, "I'll tell him and do the paperwork for shipment tomorrow."

André Lebeau was not *beau* at all. A rumpled fat man, late-forties with messy long brown hair, bad complexion and squinty eyes. He looked sleazy. He was sleazy. His three computer stores were renowned for selling at the lowest prices in town and for doing cash under the table. He squeezed his suppliers to the bone, but he was hard to ignore and occasionally gave Dale orders that were worth taking. The price he wanted to pay was always painful to accept and Dale didn't trust him, so he kept Lebeau on tight terms.

Dale had arrived at *InfoCité* on Sainte Catherine Street East before seven o'clock. It was his habit to arrive earlier than expected for any scheduled meeting. It was partly his obsessive nature and partly for any advantage he might gain. *InfoCité* was in a part of town that Dale was still getting to know. He was after all, English, living and working in the West Island suburbs. The eastern sections of the city were not exactly foreign to him, but they were far from his familiar neighborhoods. The store was east of Saint Laurent Boulevard, the recognized dividing line between the French and English communities in Montreal. *La rue Sainte Catherine* was the major west-to-east street that sliced across Montreal from the suburb of Westmount, with its stone mansions on the hillside above the Canadiens' hockey arena, called the Forum, through the city centre with its high office towers and major department stores, flashy boutiques, movie theatres, clubs and restaurants, continuing east across Saint Laurent Boulevard to the less glamorous shops, bars and strip joints in the well-worn buildings of Montreal's 1950s heyday.

InfoCité was a brightly lit store on the corner. The racks and shelves full of computer products inside were exposed through large windows covered by thick steel bars to discourage break-ins. Dale went into the store and wandered down the aisle checking the products on display.

He approached the cashier.

"*Bonsoir, comment ça va?* How are you this evening?"

The pimply young man took a moment to disengage from his *Journal de Montreal.*

"*Je peux vous aider?*"

"*J'ai une rencontre avec André Lebeau.* He's expecting me."

"*Il n'est pas ici,*" the clerk replied, "*Il est dans son appartement.*"

He tipped his head toward the side door and hallway leading up the stairs to Lebeau's apartment, "He's upstairs."

"*Merci,*" said Dale. The kid went back to his newspaper.

Dale walked out of the store up the stairs to the landing and started through the open door to the apartment. He looked down the narrow hall past closed doors on either side and saw André Lebeau sitting at the kitchen table in a loosely-slung green Terry-towel bathrobe. Dale knocked on his way in and went down the hall. André turned toward him exposing his naked belly hanging over white underwear.

Jesus, I am going to have to kiss his ugly fat ass, thought Dale.

Disgusting as it was, he pulled up a chair, pushed some dirty dishes and an overflowing ashtray aside and slid the invoice toward André.

"*Bonjour André*, thanks for the nice order," he said.

"*Pas de problème*," said André, as he pulled a big manila envelope across the table, exposing bundles of cash inside. "*Mais, j'paie pas le plein montant.*"

"What do you mean you're not paying the full amount?"

"*Tu m'as couté trop cher avec CSA.*"

"What are you talking about? How did I cost you money?"

"*Je l'explique en anglais, mon ami, juste pour toi.*" Squinting at Dale, he explained in English.

"I discover it was you, who report about my new monitors not CSA approved."

CSA was the Canadian Standards Association responsible for ensuring that all products sold in Canada met the necessary safety standards. Like UL, the Underwriter's Laboratory for the insurance industry in the U.S., they inspected and approved product design, components and construction to ensure there were no risks of fire or electrical shock. It could be a frustrating bureaucratic obstacle that forced long delays on the introduction of new products to the market, especially for the increasing number of imported electronic and computer products from questionable sources off shore. André Lebeau was not alone in skipping the CSA approval process in order to expedite sales.

"I didn't know you were the importer, André." Dale shrugged. "My sales rep found them at a dealer who stopped buying our monitors. The rep told me there was no CSA sticker on them, so I reported it. You know it's not legal to sell product without CSA approval. Sometimes that cheap shit you're buying blows up on the customer or sets his place on fire. You should play by the rules, André."

"*Piff.* You never win playing by the rules. Anyway, the inspector come here and he want me to get the product approved and pay a big fine, too."

"Sorry about that."

"No problem, I made a deal with him for cash. He told me it was you that reported it."

"You solve a lot of problems with cash, André. Now let's solve this one for only $37,343 dollars."

"*Bonne idée. Mais, ... pas trop vite.* Not so fast, Dale. I think a good price for one hundred of your monitors is $35,000. Then we have a deal."

Dale clenched his teeth. It was still an acceptable price to move some surplus stock, but he hated being squeezed again after the deal was done.

"I don't like changing the price after we've agreed on it," he said after a few seconds. "But, OK this time, André, since I caused you a little trouble with CSA." He smiled to himself. "Let's do it."

"*Excellent!* At that price I take fifty more. *Attends,* wait a minute." He poked at his calculator, then turned it toward Dale. "That makes $52,500, *eh?*"

Dale nodded.

André reached for the envelope, pulled out a stack of $1000 bills and started peeling them off. Dale said nothing and watched André count. At least he was picking up a good bundle of cash for his own purposes. There was a bright side, even in this sleazy apartment.

Dale remembered he had gone straight to the bank the next morning to deposit some of the cash and put the rest in the locked safe at home. He was beginning to feel a little sleazy himself with all the cash he was moving around, but he was getting used to the concept.

***

"Dale," Susan said, "Did you even notice? Keira just scored again."

He jumped up and cheered.

"Way to go, Keira!" He sat back down and looked at Susan.

"Sorry, my mind wandered a little. But yes, I did notice, she's having a great game. And her skating is getting much better. You should find a girl's hockey team for her. I think she's ready. Maybe she's the next hockey player in the family."

Susan was shaking her head.

"No way. Ringette's fine for her. She'll appreciate you showing up though, nice to see you get away from the office for a change. Everything under control?"

"Yeah, pretty much. And we're having a great month. Getting away is a good idea though, time to start thinking about summer holiday plans."

They both turned back to the action on the ice.

7.

The drab grey street and somber sky were only slightly brightened by the patches of wet snow on the parked cars and sidewalks several blocks east of the retail strip where *InfoCité* was located. The black Cadillac Seville was parked opposite a dingy bar with a faded wooden sign on the wall that read *Taverne Leblanc* above an illuminated red-and-white neon *Molson Export* sign.

It was a quiet afternoon. Inside, there was only one drinker at the bar and two more at the tables scattered across the open room beneath dangling yellow glass light shades.

Frank the Fixer was sipping a beer, sitting back on the worn cracked leather bench seat watching Jacques Talbot fondle his girlfriend in a back corner booth. It was not a classy place and Frank would not normally hang out at a spot like this.

After a long hard kiss, Jacques got up, gave the girlfriend a squeeze good-bye and went out the door. The girlfriend straightened her tight black skirt and tied the white blouse in front exposing her ample cleavage and white belly. She strode on red-sandaled heels back to work behind the bar.

Frank waited until she looked his way and signaled her to come over and bring him another beer.

When she arrived at his booth, he moved over to give her space on the bench seat.

"Sit down a minute. I need to ask you something."

She glanced back at the other bartender, looked again at the handsome man sitting in the booth and sat down beside him.

"I noticed you earlier there with your boyfriend and I'd like to meet him. Can you tell me where he lives?"

Her expression darkened.

"No," she said and started to get up.

Frank grabbed her arm.

"I really need to know where he lives. And I want you to help me out."

He pulled her down beside him and looked straight into her eyes.

She glared at him.

"Oh yeah? Then why don't you just fuck me and I'll tell you whatever you want."

He tightened his grip.

"Believe me, if I wanted to fuck you, we'd be done by now. Just tell me what I need to know and I won't hurt you."

He moved his other hand to her thigh, yanked her closer to him in the booth and squeezed her arm until she flinched. She continued glaring at him, then spit out an apartment address in the north-east end of Montreal.

"What's his name and who does he work for?"

Frank already knew, but he was enjoying the control and squeezed her arm tighter.

She winced and hesitated again before leaning in close to his face.

"Jonnie Talbot. And he works for Gino Boncanno, who will hurt me worse than you ever could, if I tell you any more. Now fuck off and leave me alone."

She pulled away and he released her. She slid out of the booth and ran to the ladies room.

Frank looked at the other bartender who turned away and focused on the glass he was polishing. Frank tossed a few bills on the table and headed for the door.

It had been a good meeting. Talbot would now know someone was looking for him.

***

Gino Boncanno was well known to Detective Pierre Forsey and Frank the Fixer.

He had been working on the fringes of organized crime in Montreal for decades, but he didn't have the connections of the more established Sicilian families of Montreal and New York. He avoided competing with their interests by limiting his criminal activity to second-tier crimes like burglary and the protection racket. He was a small-time gangster who thought of himself as a gentleman among the ruffians in the business. He tried to be as polished and cultured as the major Mafia bosses and not as crude and aggressive as the biker gangs working the same turf, but he used all the same tactics of intimidation and violence.

Boncanno worked from a large private office at Club Calabrese in Montreal North. The Club was a conspicuously ostentatious ceramic brick and marble two-story building with bas-relief artwork around the high front entrance capped with a wrought-iron enclosed balcony. Large windows with heavy red drapes framed the spacious reception halls and dining rooms on both floors. The Club was a popular venue for family functions and events, especially the extravagant Italian wedding receptions that took place there regularly. Boncanno's office was off a large hallway that connected the private Calabrese Club facilities to the Luna Rossa Restaurant which opened on the opposite street.

Boncanno was in his office the same afternoon that Frank was having a beer on Saint Catherine Street.

He was sitting at his desk and shaking his finger at the large man, Vito D'Alessandro, standing in front of him. D'Alessandro had the over-powering size advantage, but he looked sheepish and intimidated by the angry red-faced Italian raging at him. Boncanno sat with his feet crossed and clamped tightly under his seat. He wore a three-piece suit with a white shirt and red tie that all looked uncomfortably tight on his round figure. His large bald head was fringed with white hair, but it was no halo.

"Dammit Vito, we need to be tougher on these people. They're not taking us seriously! You're letting them off too easy." His fist pounded the desktop.

"They should be afraid for their lives, then they'll find a way to pay."

He sat back and collected himself.

"OK, bring him in and we'll see he gets the message."

Vito went to the side door of Boncanno's office and opened it to wave in another heavy-set bodyguard who was gripping the arm of a small curly-haired man with his suit jacket pulled askew. The bodyguard marched him into the office, grabbed a straight-backed wooden chair from against the wall, set it in front of Boncanno's desk and slammed the man down into it. Vito came up beside the chair and placed his left hand on the man's shoulder holding him in place.

Boncanno looked at the small, sweating man and slowly shook his head.

"My friend," he said, "we had an understanding. You're supposed to pay me every week. Now you're whining you don't have the money, so we haven't been paid for two weeks. You know, that is not acceptable."

The man put his hands together and stammered.

"But, but, I just cannot pay. Maybe next week. I have no money and no one to help me. Maybe next week."

"But now your problem has become my problem. And you know that if I do not get my money, I have to take a pound of flesh, right? Like it says in the Bible."

"Please, just another week and I'll find the money."

"No." Boncanno shook his head.

"You said that last week." He looked up at Vito and nodded.

Vito slammed his right fist into the man's face and knocked him backwards onto the floor. The man rolled over onto his hands and knees beside the chair lying sideways and blood dripped from his mouth and nose.

"Not on my carpet!" screamed Boncanno. "Get him out of here!"

Vito grabbed the man by the back of his suit jacket and pulled him upright, swiping the blood off the carpet with his hand and wiping it on the man's chest. The other bodyguard placed the chair quickly back against the wall and gave the carpet another wipe with his white handkerchief. The two heavies dragged the man out and closed the door quietly behind them.

Gino took out his own handkerchief to wipe his brow and went back to leafing through the papers on his desk.

About thirty minutes later, he heard a light tap, tap and the door was held open by another burly man for a dark-haired boy in school uniform. The boy looked in.

"Hello, Papa."

Boncanno got up and opened his arms to the boy. He leaned forward and gave him a hug, held him by the shoulders and kissed him on both cheeks before lifting him up onto the desk, where he sat with his legs crossed and hands gripping the edge.

Gino sat down and rolled his chair back to look at his son.

"How was school today, Antonio?"

"Um-m-m-m, OK."

"And what did you learn today, my beautiful son?"

The boy paused, looking down and swinging his feet.

"Um-m-m-m," he replied in a small voice, "I learned I don't like Lisa Henderson."

"Oh. Why don't you like her, Antonio?"

Still looking down, he hesitated before replying.

"She said I'm a fat Wop and 'Don't touch me.'" He jerked his hand off the desk and pulled it to his chest with a pout, like Lisa Henderson had done.

Gino's own memory of schoolboy incidents hit him like a punch in the gut.

"Don't worry about it, Antonio, she's just a mean, stupid little girl. She's jealous she's not a smart, good-looking Italian like you."

He patted his son's knee and looked into Antonio's eyes.

"Did you try to touch her?"

Antonio looked up quickly.

"I just wanted to hold her hand during fire drill. We were supposed to walk out two-by-two." Then quietly again, "I thought I liked her."

Horny little toad, thought Gino. His son was already showing signs of becoming the hot-blooded Italian that he wanted him to be. And he's only ten years old. He smiled at his own memories of clumsy romantic adventures, though nothing much happened for him until high school.

"Aren't there any nice Italian girls in your class?"

"Yeah-h-h-h.... But they're all fat Wops, too."

"Antonio!"

Gino stood and put his big hands firmly around his son's small shoulders.

"Don't ever say that. We're Italian, not Wops, and proud of it. And we stick up for each other, like family."

Even if we're not always nice to each other, he thought.

"Just remember to behave and do well at school. They'll all learn to show you some respect."

And I know ways to teach them, if I need to, Gino added silently to himself.

"Do you want Mama to speak to your teacher?"

"No Papa, it's OK." Antonio slipped off the desk and hugged his father around the waist.

"I love you, son. Go on home now and I'll see you at dinner."

As the boy left, Gino rolled his chair back up to the big desk and pulled forward his inbox full of letters. He looked up at the drape-covered windows and his mind wandered back to his own past, then forward to the future for his son. His gaze came back to the papers on his desk.

On top was a letter embossed with the emblem of *La Ville de Montréal Nord*, the east-end suburb where the Club was located. It was a personal invitation from the Mayor to a fundraising event in two weeks. Gino then pulled out a more formal legal document from City Hall explaining a zoning violation related to his private parking space in front of the Luna Rossa restaurant. *A small donation and a word with the Mayor will make that go away,* he thought.

Gino kept a low profile, but maintained a friendly relationship with the local mayors and a few city councillors to avoid any unpleasant surprises. Timely gifts and donations kept them from any interference with his business. He also quietly cultivated mutually beneficial arrangements with a few friendly cops to keep their interference to a minimum.

Detective Pierre Forsey was one of those cops.

8.

Dale had been keeping a stash of cash at home and in the office to fill the envelopes for Jacques. He was also finding himself rationalizing deals for cash to keep up. It was leading to bad habits in his accounting, since he could no longer put all those transactions through the books. Losing track of his numbers was contrary to his nature.

But I've got to do what I can to survive, he thought.

Another Tuesday was approaching and the envelope with three thousand cash was locked in the reception desk at 3D Computers waiting for the next pickup. Dale was trying to focus on his work at the office and wondering if Frank the Fixer had put Jacques out of business yet. He hadn't heard anything from Frank and he was nervous about contacting Forsey again. The threats to his family still had him on edge.

The intercom buzzed.

"Dale," said Marie, "It's Mr. Petrie from the bank on line two."

Rick Petrie was the Manager at the *Montréal Banque de Commerce* responsible for the account of 3D Computers. He had been very helpful with the initial financing, when Dale first opened his business and then again when he bought out his partners.

Petrie had arranged the floating line of credit that allowed Dale the financing he needed to pay his off-shore suppliers and carry the inventory until it was sold and customer payments were received. As sales grew, the required financing had increased substantially. The credit limit was now up to $1.5 million, but it had to be supported by sufficient value in inventory and accounts receivable each month to provide adequate security for the bank. It was a standard banking arrangement that required 3D Computers to submit financial reports each month-end to confirm the values and re-calculate the allowed credit limit for the following month.

Dale picked up line two.

"Hi Rick, what's new? Did I win another award for fastest growing customer at the branch?"

"Not yet Dale, but I have noticed you're still growing fast and maybe that's the problem. You seem to need rescue from a tight cash situation."

"What do you mean?"

"Well, I'm looking at a check here for just over $76,000 that has been flagged to be returned for insufficient funds."

"Jesus, don't return the check! Nothing kills a credit rating like a bounced check and I don't ever want to do that to a supplier."

"I understand Dale, but this check takes you more than $20,000 over your current credit limit of $1,375,000. That's all the receivables and inventory can support, based on your last month-end financials."

"I know, but I need to keep my suppliers working with me, Rick, not make them nervous about getting paid."

"Don't worry, Dale, I'll sign off if you can cover it quickly, but I don't know what else is coming and I thought you should know how tight you are."

Oh, I know, thought Dale.

"Great. I appreciate you taking care of it. I'm sure we're good. Sales are booming with government year-end. I'll bring you updated statements tomorrow and they should cover us right up to the limit of $1.5 million. Sorry to make you worry for nothing."

"All right. Sounds good. Come and see me tomorrow about three-thirty. But Dale, please don't get too creative with those statements. I need to be able to share them here and keep my credibility too."

"Absolutely. No problem."

Dale hung-up and let out a long breath. He knew exactly what the problem was and he was prepared to get sufficiently creative to satisfy the bank and look after his need for cash at the same time.

A big order from Civil Systems in Ottawa had been delivered over two months ago and they were refusing to pay the invoice of $480,000. The whole shipment had been delivered to one Federal Government department and the systems manager there had decided that the product failed to meet specifications. Not the industry standard, nor the previously accepted computer monitor product specifications, but his personal wish list. Dale thought it was bullshit, of course, but the government was holding back payment and so was Civil Systems. Dale was scheduled to visit Ottawa on Thursday with Guy Tremblay, his Technical Services Manager, and settle the issues in order to get paid, but now he had to satisfy his banker first. Tomorrow was Tuesday.

He went down the hall to see his Office Manager, Monique Chevrier. She could help with the creative accounting necessary to bump up the credit limit and get 3D past this temporary obstacle. In fact, Dale thought, they should probably make some changes in the reported numbers to keep the loan at the maximum of $1.5 million.

He walked into Monique's office, lost in thought as he moved two chairs and her small conference table into the corner, then plunked himself down in the armchair facing her desk and waited for her to disengage from the computer screen full of spreadsheets and charts. She glanced sideways at him, finished entering some data, hit 'Save' and then turned to face him.

Monique looked more like a fashion model than an accountant. Meticulously manicured finger nails, long waves of blonde hair, a pretty pink mouth and light green eyes, she wore a silky white blouse and short grey skirt exposing long legs and black high-heels that she crossed and tucked under her desk.

"You look a little frazzled, Dale."

"We're under a little pressure. Rick Petrie just called with the news that we're over our credit limit and he's ready to start returning checks."

"He wouldn't dare! He loves having our account."

"He does, but he has bosses too. And unfriendly computers looking over his shoulder checking our numbers. There's only so much he can do."

"*Maudit, ce sont les cochons chez Civile Systèmes.*"

Dale laughed.

"You're right and I'm cursing them too, but it's not nice to call them pigs, Monique."

He appreciated that she was on top of the situation and she was fiercely protective of 3D Computers.

"But we need to love and respect our customers, even when they piss us off and treat us like shit," Dale said.

"OK, but can you please stop re-arranging my furniture. It gets annoying, you know."

Dale continued.

"I'm going to Ottawa Thursday with Guy to sort out the technical issues and get our money, but I promised to bring Petrie financial statements tomorrow that support the $1.5 million credit limit."

"But they don't."

"They will tomorrow. Let me explain how we're going to do that."

Dale knew that Monique understood how the credit limit was determined by the combined values of accounts receivable and inventory on-hand.

"So we need to increase both those amounts on the balance sheet. First I want you to find some orders not yet shipped, that we can invoice now. Invent some if you have to, just try to make them plausible, in case we have to explain them to an auditor. We can reverse them later, if necessary. Don't tell me too much, so I can explain it as an innocent mistake, not something I asked for."

"That sounds a long way from the accounting principles I learned at *l'Université de Montréal*."

"Not really. I think we're still legal, just a little more creative than the average accountant. It's the engineer in me."

He tapped the iron ring on the little finger of his right hand that was the traditional symbol of a Canadian engineering graduate, then wiggled his pinky at Monique.

"Now, on the inventory, I want you to start adding in all the product that's on the water."

"How is that legal?" She looked skeptical.

"Well, I actually checked that with our good buddy, Morrie Schneider," Dale said.

"He's a creative accountant who always keeps us legal and he knows all about imports from his rag-trade clients. Morrie explained that since we actually pay for the product FOB in the Far East, meaning as soon as it's on board the ship, then it's legitimate to recognize the inventory in transit among our assets. That's why we insure it from that point on. It's our product and not the shipper's problem, if we lose it at sea."

"OK, got it," said Monique. She looked at a shipping schedule on her desk and ran her finger down the list of incoming containers.

"We must have two or three containers *en route*, so that'll add at least $400,000 and raise the limit by $200,000, maybe more."

"You catch on quick, Monique. That's what I like about you."

He turned and started for the door without touching her furniture.

"And you thought it was the great legs," he added.

She smiled, shaking her head slowly, and turned back to her computer screen.

***

Later that evening a few miles east in the north end of the city, Jacques Talbot pulled his Dodge Ram pickup into the parking space outside his apartment building. The black Caddy that had been behind him for the last few blocks rolled up into the space beside him.

The driver of the Caddy was a wide-shouldered young black man, who got out and opened Jacques' passenger door. He climbed in and placed his large hand on the dashboard.

"Nice truck."

"Who the hell are you?"

Jacques was thinking this must be the guy he had heard about from his girlfriend. He ran his eyes over the hard-muscled body in his passenger seat.

Frank turned to face him and spoke in a quiet, low voice.

"I'm the guy who is *not* going to kill you for Gino Boncanno."

"What!"

"C'mon Jonnie, you knew this couldn't last and it was going to end badly. Gino doesn't like his hired help working on the side and using his name for leverage. He wants to hurt you just to send a message."

Jacques stared at him with clamped jaw, thinking fast. There was no denying it, he was in trouble. He thought, *how the hell did Gino find out about my little side business? How the fuck do I get out of this now?*

"Look," he said, "I can give Gino his percentage. I can give him a hundred percent."

"Too late for that, Jacques. But he doesn't want me to kill you, so you're actually getting off easy."

Frank let Jacques think about that for a few seconds.

"Let me tell you what we're going to do with you and your truck."

Jacques thought about the gun in the glove compartment in front of Frank and the switchblade in his pocket.

In a flash, Frank's hand shot out and seized Jacques' wrist in a tight grip, holding his hand against the steering wheel.

"Don't do anything foolish. Gino doesn't want you dead, but I don't really care."

Frank's speed and power were very persuasive. The low voice made him seem even more intimidating. Jacques didn't need a more painful demonstration of Frank's capabilities and silently decided to cooperate.

Frank pulled a mickey of whisky out of his jacket pocket and handed it to Jacques.

"You're going to drink at least half of this right now and then we're going for a drive. Fasten your seatbelt."

***

Winter in Montreal means an accumulation of snow and ice, anytime from late November to mid-March. City maintenance crews are well equipped to plow and salt the city streets, roads and highways to keep them clear and safe. Nevertheless, it can be hazardous driving anywhere.

That evening a salesman driving home late on the elevated Metropolitan Expressway was suddenly alarmed to see two vehicles in his rear view mirror approaching rapidly and weaving erratically across the three lanes.

He pulled to the right, careful to avoid the icy snow bank pushed up against the guard rail and slowed to let them pass. He saw that one vehicle was a red pickup and the other was a black sedan. They seemed to be racing each other. As they passed in the two lanes beside him, he saw the sedan in the far left lane veer towards the pickup.

"Oh, my God!"

The pickup jerked right, mounted the frozen snow bank and launched over the guardrail into the air above the street below, then plunged out of sight.

The salesman slowed down and checked his mirror for any more trouble behind him. He grabbed his car phone from the bracket attached to the center console and punched 9-1-1.

"There's been an accident on the Met near Christophe Coulombe and a pickup just jumped the guard rail! It must've landed on the service road going west."

The operator said she would dispatch police and emergency vehicles and asked him to go back and tell the police what he saw. He hung up and headed for the next exit down to the service road so he could circle back to the spot where he had seen the pickup go over the railing.

He did a second U-turn under the Met to come back along the west-bound service road and drove slowly up to the scene where he saw a red Dodge Ram pick-up smashed into the pavement, lying on its passenger side with two police cars and an ambulance pulled up behind it, lights flashing. Nothing else had been hit, but there were two other cars parked along the service road with three people standing alongside gawking at the wreck. The *Urgences Santé* ambulance attendants were trying to extricate the driver from the pickup.

The salesman walked up to one of the cops directing traffic to a side street.

"I saw it from the Met up there."

He pointed above their heads to a twisted piece of steel railing that was sticking out into the dark between the street lights.

"He was racing another car, a black sedan, I think, that ran him into the side and he flew right over the guard rail."

The officer asked him some more questions and wrote in his notebook before slipping it into his vest pocket.

"I don't know about the other car, but this guy had been drinking for sure. Lucky he didn't kill himself or somebody else."

They didn't notice the black Caddy parked on the side street half a block away. The still silhouette of the wide-shouldered driver was watching the scene on the service road.

***

The bank had been satisfied with the updated financials that Dale presented and had raised the credit line up to the maximum of $1.5 million. Now the hold-up in Ottawa had to be settled.

The National Capital was just over a two-hour drive from the office in Montreal on the TransCanada Highway across the border into the province of Ontario. Dale was driving with Guy Tremblay beside him and two monitors on the backseat. Dale had learned that neither the QPP, the Quebec Provincial Police called *la Sûreté du Québec*, nor the OPP, the Ontario Provincial Police, were very tolerant of speeding on the TransCanada, so he kept it under 120 kilometres-an-hour. It was also marked on his speedometer as 75 miles-per-hour, even though Prime Minister Pierre Trudeau had thrown out Imperial measure with other remnants of the British Empire in his personal political mission to declare Canada independent of Olde England. Many of Trudeau's policies were still unpopular in Western Canada and his initiatives hadn't stopped the separatists from wanting to leave the country, but most of the population still loved him. Cocky, flamboyant, articulate and outspoken in both languages, not at all the quiet Canadian stereotype. The more arrogant and even less popular current Prime Minister, Brian Mulroney, had left most of Trudeau's Canadian nationalist policies intact.

An excursion to the National Capital of Ottawa always caused Dale to reflect on Canadian politics, but it was not a topic for discussion with Guy Tremblay who had strong feelings about protecting Quebec's interests and probably separatist sympathies. They talked instead about the challenges of the technology business and unreasonable customer expectations encouraged by the unceasing stream of new products with levels of performance that current products simply couldn't meet. That analysis of the situation was part of their planned pitch to Civil Systems in Ottawa.

Civil Systems specialized in Federal Government contracts and did very well installing and upgrading systems for the dozens of departments and several hundred thousand civil servants in Ottawa. Their large office building in an industrial park on the eastern edge of the city had a well-equipped technical centre and a small warehouse. Civil Systems had no consumer retail outlets and the company President, Paul Gosselin, had explained his reasoning to Dale in the past.

"Civil servants in Ottawa have lots of money to spend on the latest computers and high tech toys, but they have too much time on their hands and waste everyone else's time while they shop around for the lowest price in town. Selling retail is just not worth the trouble. Government and corporate purchasing agents have a lot more money to spend and they make it worth our while to baby them along."

And if Civil Systems did well, so did Dale. It was worth babying them along too, he thought, but this hold-up of $480,000 over an imagined defect in the product was too much to take from even the best of customers.

They were ushered into a large conference room and Dale put a file folder neatly in front of his chair, then walked over to the window and stared outside re-thinking his approach to negotiating this dilemma to the right conclusion. Guy opened his briefcase and placed a pile of thick files on the table with print-outs and engineering spec sheets sliding out sideways.

The door opened and Paul Gosselin walked in, followed by Terry Fitzgerald, his Sales Manager and Pierre Tessier, his Technical Services Manager.

"Hi, Dale," said Gosselin, "Thanks for coming to help us get this problem solved."

After handshakes and introductions, they all sat down and got settled in their places. Dale spoke up immediately.

"Before we get started, let me repeat what I said on the phone Monday, Paul. There is no goddamn way I'll accept threats of non-payment over this issue. We delivered what was ordered and we expect to get paid, as agreed. Any technical issues we'll deal with separately. Is that understood?"

Guy Tremblay looked down and focused on his files. Fitzgerald and Tessier, on the other side of the table, looked stunned.

Paul Gosselin replied calmly.

"I understand, Dale, but as I told you on the phone, this is not a threat. We cannot pay, because they will not pay. I know you think their guy is an incompetent asshole, but he needs to be satisfied before his boss will release payment. So let's get our shit together and get over there to make that happen. They're expecting us at two o'clock."

Dale gestured to Guy's pile of documents.

"We're ready to prove that his complaint about misalignment is bullshit. We have two perfect specimens in the car, to shove up his ass if necessary."

He looked at Gosselin.

"Don't worry," Dale said, "I'll be more polite when we meet him. I don't want to blow off your customer either, Paul, at least not until we all get paid. But I have to leave here today with a check. I have a banker I need to keep happy."

The long meeting that afternoon with senior bureaucrats and the Director of Procurement tested Dale's diplomacy and his patience. He had to engage in long technical explanations and demonstrate the EXL display alignment compared to two other monitors made by HP and Viewsonic that they pulled off desktops outside the conference room. The misalignment was worse on the Viewsonic and only slightly better on the HP. Guy Tremblay couldn't resist explaining that alignment was a challenge for all manufacturers, since they had to calibrate and adjust the deflection coils inside the tube depending on the intended destination and its location relative to the magnetic north pole. Dale thought it might be more than they needed to know, but decided that overwhelming them with technical information was helping to convince them of their competence and to get acceptance of the monitors they had delivered.

Dale and Guy left at the end of the day with satisfied customers all around and an initial check from Civil Systems for $75,000. The rest would be settled over the following two weeks.

It shouldn't be this hard, Dale thought, with customers and criminals all trying to take a piece of him. His accumulated anger and frustration showed on the way back to Montreal.

Guy Tremblay watched anxiously as the speedometer stayed well over 130 kilometers-an-hour for long stretches of highway in the dark, but they made it home without a speeding ticket.

9.

Another week went by without hearing any more about protection money or Jacques Talbot. The envelope of cash still sat untouched in the drawer, so Dale decided to go ahead with his planned trip to Korea and Taiwan. It would be his fourth trip and he was not looking forward to it.

His first trip to assess his preferred suppliers for EXL monitors two years earlier had been an education for the young man a long way from his old home town in the Canadian Rockies.

The first trip started with a short hop from Montreal to Toronto. Dale was joined there by his two business partners, Don Leeman and Doug Maxwell, for the two-hour Air Canada flight to Chicago. From Chicago, they flew Korean Air Lines to Seoul on a fourteen-hour non-stop flight that was a long-distance endurance test. Almost three hundred bored passengers, American and Korean businessmen, women and children, all crowded inside a narrow aluminum cylinder with insufficient food, drink or movies to escape from the ordeal. Even the memory of KAL Flight 007 from New York City to Seoul that had been shot down just three years earlier by the Soviets, claiming it was a spy plane and killing all 269 people aboard, wasn't enough to add any excitement en route.

Don Leeman and Doug Maxwell were more accustomed to the long-distance flight, as they had already been several times to the Far East to visit manufacturers and agents for their other imports from Korea and Taiwan. Their methodology to endure the ordeal was essentially to sit still, sleep, eat and enjoy the free booze until they finally staggered off the plane.

Don and Doug were still investors in 3D Computers on that first trip, then continued to accompany Dale on later trips after they were no longer partners, but still joint customers of the two manufacturers. Dale appreciated their assistance with both the product technical specifications and the complex negotiations on pricing, terms and conditions. Their management style and their approach to sales and marketing were very different from Dale's, but they still made a valuable contribution. They, in turn, appreciated the creativity and the profitability that Dale added to their own businesses.

On arrival in Korea, Dale had never been so dazed and disoriented from jet lag as he was for those first few days in Seoul. He found the continuous eating and drinking that were part of the hospitality arrangements seemed to help him recover though.

The two manufacturers that Dale had selected for EXL monitors were Korea Computer Systems in Seoul, known as KCS, owned by the brothers Jay and Danny Koh, and Chung-Wai in Taipei, owned by Sammy Wong.

On his first visit, Dale had discovered that the owners of the two companies were both fiercely ambitious and patriotic, determined to win business not only for their companies, but also for their countries, Korea and Taiwan. The competition for the increasingly attractive orders from Canada worked to the advantage of the three business partners.

Dale consistently succeeded in negotiating more favorable pricing and bigger concessions from the two manufacturers than the big multinationals that he was competing with in North America. The multinationals lost their size advantage and any loyalty from the suppliers by insisting on new price quotations every year and frequently switching to new suppliers. Dale and his associates instead made it clear that they would buy only from KCS and Chung-Wai, unless they were forced to go elsewhere because of unacceptable prices or poor product quality. Those tactics were very effective at keeping their costs competitive and the manufacturers responsive to their constantly changing demands.

Doug Maxwell was the engineering expert on the team with the most knowledge of computer technology. It was his role to ensure that both manufacturers met industry standard technical specifications and the quality and reliability criteria that they set for EXL monitors.

Dale's role was to work on the marketing and sales plans and develop strategies for introducing products to the computer retailers and systems integrators. They all used the same EXL packaging and promotional materials that he designed, but Dale was by far the most successful at selling in his market of Quebec and Eastern Canada and consistently surpassed his associates' sales numbers in Toronto, even though they served a larger market. Dale was expecting them to make a proposal soon for him to assume responsibility for their sales in Ontario and Western Canada, but for now, he had enough challenges in Montreal.

If he could get off the hook for protection money and negotiate better terms with the suppliers to relieve the stress on his financing, perhaps he would raise the subject himself.

During that first trip, Doug Maxwell had given Dale his initial basic training in computer monitors. In the mid-1980s, monitors were simple displays using a CRT or cathode ray tube, similar to the glass picture tube that had been used in television sets since the 1950s. Instead of a TV broadcast signal, however, the computer monitor received a video signal directed by software through the graphics card and electronics to display images on the screen.

"Think of it like a little man sitting inside at the back of the tube with a flashlight that he switches on and off sixty times a second to illuminate the phosphor on the inside of the tube." Doug explained. "If it's a monochrome monitor, the phosphor is amber or green like the standard computer terminals or white, which is now getting more popular for personal computer applications like VisiCalc and Lotus 1-2-3 for spreadsheets and Word Star or Word Perfect for word-processing."

"OK, but what about color monitors," Dale asked.

"That's a little more complicated," said Doug. "First, the phosphor is arranged in three-color dots of red, green and blue. That's why it's called an RGB monitor. Now the little man with the flashlight has to be even smarter, faster and more accurate to hit the right mix of colors for complex color-graphics displays. There's actually a metal screen inside the CRT that helps focus the electron beam in a color monitor. The finer the screen, the higher the resolution for sharper detail in the display."

Dale shook his head.

"You remember I'm really not a very competent engineer, right? I hope you don't expect me to understand or remember all this technology mumbo-jumbo."

"Just so long as you know more than the customer and sell a lot of 'em," said Doug. "All the dealers care about is price, anyway. A little mumbo-jumbo will make you sound like a real monitor expert, which is what we're supposed to be, after all."

"You think we could make them a little better looking?" Dale said. "They all look the same in those boring beige plastic cases."

"Not a good idea for us," said Doug. "Apple and IBM have got us all hooked on boring beige. You might see some grey or black coming soon, but we don't want to take a chance on trying it first. Our strategy is simple remember, same as the big guys, only cheaper."

"Sounds simple," said Dale.

"Yeah, but the technology business is like the fucking fashion industry, Dale. Everybody wants to have what's coming next. And the new product developments just never stop. Soon you'll see the end of these ugly heavy CRT monitors. They'll be replaced by the new flat screen displays being developed in Japan. They use liquid crystal displays called LCDs, or light-emitting diodes called LEDs. In a few years, that's all we'll be selling. I hope KCS and Chung-Wai are able to keep up when we have to compete with that technology."

Dale had done very well selling a lot with limited technical knowledge, but he did worry about the rapid changes in technology and the fickle customers. He didn't like the strategy of simply selling on lowest price. That's why he worked so hard on the product packaging, design and marketing materials to support higher prices and better profit margins. It had taken him a while to convince the other two engineers, Don and Doug, that marketing and good salesmanship actually worked. It was never as simple as 'same product, lower price.'

He was convinced that customers always assumed that a higher price meant better product and it was a lot easier to raise the price to premium levels and 'sell like hell,' than it was to build a premium product. Dale's marketing strategy was entirely dependent on his two suppliers, KCS and Chung-Wai, who were both competent manufacturers, but definitely second-tier, not premium.

Doing business in Korea and Taiwan was very different from Dale's prior experience in North America and Europe. The business agendas always covered the same essential issues related to product specifications, sales forecasts, pricing and shipping schedules, but in Korea and Taiwan the formal meetings were limited to brief interruptions in the non-stop hospitality and partying that lasted from their initial arrival until their final departure. The competition between suppliers was as much about who could be the best host, as it was about who could offer the best product at the best price.

The three Canadians were escorted everywhere by the business owners and their senior management associates, in both Korea and Taiwan. In Korea they enjoyed long lunches together followed by a formal dinner every evening. The meals usually started with a spicy hot pot of noodles and vegetables, followed by large plates filled with tender chunks of beef, chicken or pork in a steaming sauce spread over a bed of rice. Dale was intrigued by the strong flavors and exotic menus, but discovered that the food gave him fits of coughing and sneezing until his palate finally adapted. His hosts tried to relieve his apparent distress by ordering the dishes with fewer of the hottest ingredients.

During the evenings, the three businessmen were introduced to their designated female companions, who were even more attentive to the needs of the visitors. In both Korea and Taiwan, it seemed to be the tradition for wealthy businessmen to have weekday mistresses. Apparently that arrangement was acceptable to their wives, who only expected the husbands to be home with the family on weekends. Jay Koh complained that the tradition had been questioned by the wives after they had lived in the United States with their families while studying at the universities there.

“They listened to all the American wives bitching about their husbands’ affairs and it was very hard to persuade them to let us have our girlfriends again, when we came back home.”

In spite of his complaint, they had happily reinstated the practice.

The female companions were made available to favored customers overnight for whatever pleasures they preferred. It was rumored that the president of a well-known American company had enjoyed the pleasure of his Korean companion in Seoul so much that he brought her back to Texas with him. His wife there was probably not quite so accepting of the Korean tradition.

Dale noticed that Don and Doug, who normally did everything together, managed to slip away separately after dinner and not explain how they had spent the night, when everyone reconvened for breakfast at the hotel in the morning.

The only explanation ever offered was a quick comment by Don Leeman.

"I hope they forgive us for our indiscretions while we're here, but surely we cannot insult the cultural traditions of our fine Korean hosts."

Dale was not at all comfortable in Korea or Taiwan with the assumption that his companion for the evening could also be his for the night. He declined to take advantage of the opportunity and eventually his hosts stopped making the offer.

One evening in Seoul during that first visit, the plentiful eating and drinking continued until Dale was starting to fade away and he was seeking an excuse to call it a night when the Kohs suggested they all retire with the girls to a private room downstairs. It was karaoke time.

A sound system and standing mic were set up in front of the sofas and lounge chairs and the two Koreans launched into their enthusiastic amateur performances. Dale would never forget joining Jay Koh in a loud drunken duet of Elvis Presley's *Love Me Tender.* Copious quantities of Passport Whisky reduced his inhibitions. Unfortunately, the large volumes of booze and spicy food made

Dale very sick in the night and very hung over for the factory visit the next day.

In the morning, they were picked up by Jay Koh at the hotel in a luxurious chauffeur-driven Hyundai sedan. Danny Koh remained in Seoul. It was a comfortable two-hour drive to the KCS factory south-east of Seoul in the small industrial city of Daegu, close to the port at Busan. It was a large sprawling property with low flat-roofed bunkhouses for the workers along the chain-link fence on one side with the monotonous grey manufacturing complex filling the rest of the property. The production workers all wore light blue KCS uniforms and tended to their tasks with military precision. The array of roller conveyers throughout the production area moved assemblies from the wave soldering machines fixing electronic components on circuit boards to the assembly area for the complete monitor, then on to the packaging and shipping areas. On the loading dock, they saw monitor boxes strapped on wooden pallets and labelled for Data General being transferred by forklift into a 40-foot container for shipment to the United States.

The last day of the visit to KCS, they relaxed with the Koh brothers at their exclusive men's club in Seoul. They wandered naked through the spa, wrapped in large thick white towels, and lounged in the ceramic-tiled rooms equipped with hot and cold water pools, some with bubbling water jets and some without, private shower rooms and bath tubs, steam rooms and saunas. There were separate private salons within the spa where attentive young ladies provided full body massages of all styles, some with a happy ending, some without.

***

On arrival in Taipei, Dale and his partners were met by a chauffeured Mercedes that brought them directly to meet Sammy Wong at Chung-Wai and Dale's orientation experience continued for another four days of business meetings and hospitality.

The serious negotiating sessions were again brief to avoid interfering with the social agenda. They had lunches delivered to the Chung-Wai conference room and relaxed over talk of current technologies and plans for future product development. Sammy was very proud of the prototype LCD flat-screen monitor that he brought into the conference room. It was an attractive, sleek, grey space-age design, but there were some 'technical issues' with the electronics. It didn't work.

"Maybe next visit we have a working prototype," said Sammy. "You like it? Very good looking, eh? And very good price."

There was no karaoke after dinner in Taiwan, but Sammy and his Sales Manager, Tommy Lee, brought them to the Taipei nightclubs for disco dancing. Sammy had arranged in advance for his guests to receive special attention from their assigned dance partners. The business issues were set aside and forgotten for the evening. It was loud and energetic and Dale was gradually loosening up to the lifestyles of wealthy businessmen in the Far East.

During his first visit to Taipei, Dale had found it unusual that Sammy twice excused himself to go to the barber shop for an hour. Don and Doug had exchanged knowing glances each time Sammy left and they all patiently waited for him to return to the meetings. It was only on the flight home, that Dale finally realized the relaxed and contented look on Sammy's face upon his return from the barber shop had nothing to do with any haircut.

***

On the way back to Toronto and Montreal, Dale reflected on what he had learned on that first visit. Korea and Taiwan were less foreign and exotic than he had expected. Both countries had adopted Western ways, from blue jeans and running shoes to Hollywood movies and fast food franchises. They were considered third-world developing economies, but they both had the look of America in their modern shopping centers with McDonald's and Kentucky Fried Chicken restaurants and Blockbuster video stores.

Taipei in Taiwan and Seoul in South Korea, however, were also very different from each other. Taipei was hyperactive, loud and polluted with narrow crowded streets between the old low-rise buildings and had rough, narrow winding roads leading out to the industrial areas. The streets were packed with small noisy cars, scooters and motorbikes belching black smoke and the occasional silent Mercedes moving down the street parting heavy traffic like the waves in front of an ocean liner. Most of the scooter and motorbike drivers and many of the pedestrians wore face masks to avoid choking on the pollution.

Seoul was a rapidly expanding modern, progressive city replacing old historic areas with high rise office towers and wide landscaped boulevards along the river through the city. Smooth wide freeways wound out to the industrial towns and port cities to the south. The cars were newer models and mostly Korean, made by Hyundai, Kia and others that Dale had not yet seen in North America.

Looking back, he thought the two cities were comparable in character to Montreal and Toronto. One was vibrant, brash and noisy with old streets and buildings in need of repair, roads and highways crowded with older cars and the other was flashy, prosperous and modern with sprawling freeways weaving through the high rise towers and jammed with expensive luxury cars.

Most of the people he had met in Korea and Taiwan were educated in the States and did business in English in the American style. Except for the extended hospitality, partying and female escorts.

Dale had learned none of this in MBA School.

***

By this fourth trip to Taiwan and Korea, Dale had become accustomed to the exhausting routine. He did not enjoy all of it, especially not the jet lag and the tiresome days of marathon eating, drinking and partying long into the night. His hosts insisted on socializing as part of every visit and Dale was too polite to refuse.

On every visit, Dale's objective was to drive down product costs and push for the latest technology from both Chung-Wai and KCS.

On this trip, however, Dale also wanted to find some relief for his cash flow challenges from his suppliers. It was difficult to finance continuing sales growth when both suppliers required a bank letter of credit to guarantee payment before they even manufactured the product. That meant Dale's line-of-credit at the bank was reduced by the value of each shipment, anywhere from $175,000 to $350,000 for each container depending on the product mix, for up to three months before the inventory was even available for sale in Montreal. It was a burden on financing that he wanted to reduce by negotiating better terms. Trust was the issue.

Dale's secondary goal on this trip was to explore some of Sammy Wong's techniques for relieving stress.

During one afternoon in Taipei, Don and Doug had decided to go shopping for souvenirs. It was a popular diversion for them in Korea and Taiwan. They both loved to boast about the bargains they found and the prices they negotiated on cheap knock-offs of luxury brand names. Nike running shoes for only $29, Rolex watches for $50 and Prada or Gucci fashions at ninety percent off their normal prices. Apparently, it helped the two men erase their guilt from behaving badly, if they bought their wives cheap souvenirs.

Dale was certain that Susan would not be so easily satisfied by fake luxury goods. Even real luxury at full price would not buy him out of the trouble he'd be in, if she caught him cheating on her, anywhere, anytime, anyhow. No explanation of cultural differences or the need to respect local customs would be sufficient to get him out of that hell-hole. He had no intention of testing his limits.

But he did need to take care of his mental health, so he declined the shopping tour and instead, agreed to go for a haircut with Sammy Wong.

It was during another round of negotiations and they all needed a break to re-consider their negotiating positions. Sammy had been very slow to deliver on their cost reduction requests, but he had been very persuasive on the value of a haircut to help Dale relax.

"You look a little tired and stressed after those long flights again, Dale," he said, "I think you really need a haircut."

Dale decided Sammy was right. It might even help negotiations with Chung-Wai. What was that line Don used about respecting their cultural traditions?

The two men were soon stretched out in a private room at the back of the barber shop that Sammy visited regularly. They lay on comfortable reclining red lounge chairs on either side of a cloth-covered partition. The lighting was subdued and the air suffused with an aroma of incense. A fountain gurgled into an aquarium along the wall below a richly colored mural with a raging dragon entangled in green vines and bright flowers leaping at the sky.

Dale thought of the two shy young ladies as geisha girls, knowing it was a Japanese term that probably did not apply in Taiwan, but assuming that the services were similar to what the geishas offered in Japan. The girls wore dark blue hot-pants and matching tight tank-tops that pushed up their small breasts. They both had flat-soled red velvet slippers and a matching red bow-tie at the throat in an attempt to evoke Playboy bunny images. No fluffy tails.

Sammy was with a short, stocky Chinese girl and Dale was watching a taller, slim girl with dyed-blonde hair leaning over to remove his trousers, pulling them out from under the white sheet she had stretched over him.

Dale tried to relax as she started to massage the muscles in his legs and work her way up to his groin. He heard Sammy moaning as he approached his happy ending. The young lady looked up at Dale before moving any further and he gave his head a quick shake to say, "No." She smiled and massaged back down his thighs and calf muscles and gestured for him to turn over. Dale found the Taiwanese haircut really was quite delightful, if he just managed to relax and focus on the pleasure with his eyes closed and his brain empty, even without the full treatment that Sammy was getting.

After the massage and a long hot soak in the steam room, he and Sammy were sitting alone together in a quiet lounge beside the massage parlour sipping fragrant floral tea and nibbling the small tasty snacks placed on china dishes in front of them. Dale didn't ask for any explanation of what was presented. He had learned previously that knowing whether it was snake or squirrel didn't make it easier to eat.

"This is a pretty good life you lead," said Dale, gesturing at the surroundings.

"Yes, it is and I enjoy it now, but it was hard work getting here. It's only the last few years that we finally broke through with the Americans. It was a big break to win the business of IBM and HP. They have been very good for us."

"Sammy, you know every manufacturer we talk to boasts about selling to IBM and HP."

"I know," said Sammy with a laugh. "It's the lie we all agree on. Some of us even keep a few IBM and HP products in the lobby to make it look true. All the customers insist on confidentiality anyway, so we can't let anybody in to see who we're actually building for. It's easy to keep on lying."

Sammy laughed again.

"You guys are very privileged to get a plant tour when you're here."

"Right," said Dale, "Another lie you can agree on. I'm told there are companies here that even give tours of somebody else's factory, just to convince customers they're real manufacturers."

"Well, you can't read the signs in Chinese, right, so why not? We never had to do that, of course. You know we're for real."

He passed a plate of snacks and Dale took a chance on something that looked like pressed meat covered in red sauce and sprinkled with sesame seeds.

Sammy continued. "We appreciate how you and your partners are patient and work with us to make progress together, Dale. That's the best way for us all to make money in this business."

Dale thought about the big Mercedes that Sammy's chauffer had manoeuvered through the traffic to the barbershop.

"I think you're doing better than we are," he said.

"Dale, you know we give you better prices and delivery than the big guys who jerk us around every year and keep shopping for a better price. They have no loyalty and, you know, there are many ways to get the price lower, if that's all you're looking for."

Dale nodded his agreement.

"I know Sammy, but we need competitive pricing too. We're up against the major brands in the market every day back home. They may have big company overheads and marketing expenses that keep their prices high, but resellers love to take the easy sale and give their customers what they want. We have to be cheaper, sell harder and persuade them we'll take good care of them and their customers. Even then, the resellers only buy from us if they make better profit margins. That's when we can all really win at this game."

"You seem to be doing all right, Dale, judging by the number of containers we're shipping to Montreal. You only started two years ago, right?"

"Yeah, we're doing all right, but it's not easy. We still need to be sharp on pricing. I hope you can do better tomorrow when we look at the new products."

"Have some more tea?" said Sammy, without looking at Dale.

"Thanks Sammy, I enjoyed the massage too. Sorry, haircut."

They exchanged smiles. Dale leaned forward to put his tea cup down and looked up at Sammy.

"There is another subject I would like to discuss, Sammy, before we sit down again with Don and Doug. Something that's a problem for me."

He paused and thought about how to tell Sammy Wong what he needed. He didn't want to give him the impression he was in trouble. He needed to build trust and not shake his confidence. Dale continued as Sammy poured more tea.

"My sales are growing fast and it's putting a lot of pressure on me to manage the financing. It's hard for me to grow and purchase under your terms, if you insist on a guarantee of payment with a letter of credit before each order even goes into production. Can we agree to terms that allow me to pay on receipt instead? That I could handle."

"But Dale, we don't do that for any customer. Are Don and Doug asking for better terms, too?

"That's up to them. It's a bigger problem for me, Sammy. You know I'm buying a lot more than they are. I'd like to continue to grow my business and give you the orders, but I need you to work with me on the terms."

Sammy sat back in the soft cushioned chair and placed his hands in his lap.

"Will you give me some of the volume that's going to KCS, if I give you better terms?"

"Absolutely. You're already getting more than half and I'll push most of the new volume to you, if you can improve the terms."

"OK, Dale." Sammy smiled. "I want to grow my business too and you have proven to be a very good customer. Let's make it a deal. I'll accept orders from now on with payment by wire transfer instead of a letter of credit. As soon as you have a fax copy of the bill-of-lading proving the goods are ready to ship, you wire us the money. Is that better?"

"That's great, Sammy. It will free up about two months of cash flow." Dale leaned across and shook his hand. "I appreciate it, now let me buy dinner tonight."

Over the next three days of back and forth negotiations, Chung-Wai offered more aggressive cost reductions for the new models of EXL color monitors. The three partners were pleased, especially with the assurance that manufacturing costs would not be reduced by using cheaper low-quality components.

Sammy emphasized again how much they appreciated the loyalty of the three partners doing business with Chung-Wai. They respectfully accepted the compliments, but kept the pressure on Sammy by letting him know they were flying on to Seoul for meetings with KCS to negotiate prices with them, too.

The business meetings in Korea also went well.

Dale never felt quite so relaxed and comfortable dealing with the Koh brothers and he didn't raise the issue of terms of payment. Part of the difference in working with the Koreans was cultural. KCS was one of the *chaebols*, companies unique to the Korean economy that had been owned by wealthy aristocratic families for generations. The *chaebols* included large global companies, like Hyundai, Samsung and Lucky Goldstar that manufactured everything from automobiles to refrigerators and television sets, but there were dozens of second and third-tier companies that had the same tightly controlled, paternalistic management style.

Coming from that background, the Koh brothers maintained an impersonal distance from everyone outside their class, especially foreigners, and they had the confident, aloof attitude that comes with inherited wealth. The Kohs were cautious businessmen and reluctant to show much trust in their customers. Dale had the same degree of caution and lack of trust in them.

Sammy Wong and his Taiwanese business associates were much more open and personable. Like entrepreneurs everywhere else, usually without a wealthy family background giving them a head start, they built their businesses with ingenuity and dedicated hard work.

The Taiwanese style of management was a better fit for Dale.

10.

After his return from Taiwan and Korea, Dale was back in the office early in the morning catching up on sales results for the period he had been away. There was no news on his situation with Jacques Talbot. The cash was still in the drawer at the front desk.

At about ten-thirty, Marie called him on the intercom.

"Dale, I have Susan on the line, she sounds a little upset."

That got his attention. Susan did not call often and she was not easily upset. He tapped the flashing button on hold and picked up the phone.

"Dale, I just had some guy here, named Jonnie Talbot. He says he's a business friend of yours."

"Who?"

"I don't know who. Jonnie Talbot, he said. A tough looking guy. Looks like he's just been in an accident, but he said he was in the area and thought you might be home."

Shit, it sounds like Jacques, thought Dale. He shuddered and started to sweat.

"What did he want?"

"He wanted me to call and tell you he would come by the office tonight after five."

He wanted me to know that he had been to the house, thought Dale. *And now he wants to see me here alone.*

"OK, no problem, I'll be here."

"Who is this guy, Dale? Pretty nasty looking friend. Is he the one hassling you for protection money?"

"Don't worry about it, he's a bit of a tough customer, but it's not a problem. I'll look after it."

"OK, but I don't want him coming to the house again, ever!"

"Fine, I'll tell him that. See you later."

He hung up the phone, then slammed his hand on the desk. "God dammit!"

He got up to close the door and noticed Marie was looking down the hall at him. He paced in his office for a minute, then grabbed his jacket and went past Marie without looking at her, walked out the front door and got into his car. He backed out of the parking space, accelerated roughly onto the street and down to the corner where he stopped abruptly, then turned hard right down another two blocks through the industrial park. He pulled sharply into a wide parking lot, found an empty space far from the other cars and parked.

He grabbed his phone from the bracket on the center console to dial Forsey's number. Forsey wasn't in, so Dale left a message.

"It's urgent. Have him call me back."

He left his car phone number and sat stewing over various disaster scenarios. *I thought we were supposed to get rid of the sonofabitch, not have him call on my wife, dammit.*

His car phone rang and he picked it up.

"Hey, Dale, what's up?"

"God dammit, Forsey, Jacques is back. I thought you had Frank the Fixer look after him."

There was a pause, before Forsey replied.

"What happened?"

"He called himself Jonnie Talbot this time, but I'm sure it was Jacques. He was at my house this morning and he's coming to see me tonight. He must know I called you and now I'm in deep shit. What the hell happened?"

"I thought Frank took care of it for you, maybe something went wrong."

"Well, apparently Jacques, or Jonnie whatever the hell he calls himself, is a little beaten up. Frank should have finished the job on the sonofabitch, instead of just getting him pissed-off at me."

"OK, calm down. I'll see what I can find out. Do you want me to be there tonight?"

"I don't know what the hell I want, but it's a little hard to calm down when he may be coming to kill me."

"That's not his style. But he may not have good news for you."

"You're a big help Forsey, but I don't think I need you to fuck it up any more. I'll call you after our little chat this evening. If I survive."

Dale slammed the phone back into its cradle. After sitting in the car for another few minutes, he drove slowly back to the office.

"Everything OK, Dale?" asked Marie, as he came in the front door. She handed him some pink telephone message slips.

"Yeah, no problem. Susan just had a message for me, from an old friend."

He went into his office and started going through his phone messages, ignoring the questions banging inside his skull. He had to focus on business and assume he was going to survive this mess. There were too many people counting on him to let it go without a fight.

He headed back down the hall from his office for another coffee. As he arrived at the narrow counter and sink, he could smell the burnt coffee. Then he saw the empty pot.

"Jesus! Marie, are you kidding me?"

Dale was not often agitated to the point of losing it, but he was pissed.

Marie heard him from the reception desk. She hurried down the hall.

"Sorry, Dale. I don't know who's the jackass drained the pot and put it back it on the burner."

"God dammit." Dale ranted, "Do we have a bunch of spoiled kids working here? Do I still have to clean up after them and make my own goddamn coffee?"

"No, no, I'll do it," said Marie.

Dale glared at her.

"I'll have it black."

He left the cup and stalked back to his office, grumbling to himself. *It's already tough enough running a business, especially with violent criminals biting at my ass. I don't have time to waste worrying about the goddamn coffee!*

***

Later that afternoon, Dale had cooled down and was again directing his attention to business.

He checked his Day-Timer to confirm the meeting scheduled for two o'clock with Guy Tremblay, Manager of Technical Services and Patrick Jensen, the Sales Manager. Dale had his files ready for review, neatly organized on his desk. He transferred them to his small round conference table, sat down and started making notes while waiting for Guy and Patrick.

The three of them brought different approaches to any problem, but they usually agreed on the action required, in spite of occasional strong differences of opinion and Patrick's need to push for a win over Guy's point of view. Guy was a college graduate in electronics and had been with Dale since early in the first year at 3D Computer

Products. He was a valuable resource, although he was inclined to talk too much, usually in a pedantic, condescending tone toward his less technical colleagues, including Dale, but they all forgave him because of his ability to solve problems quickly before they became too costly or jeopardized sales.

Patrick Jensen was a more recent hire, who came to 3D Computers with an excellent track record and strong recommendations from his customers. Of course, that meant that Dale had to offer him a very attractive salary and bonus package to persuade him to leave a competing distributor, but Patrick was delivering major new customers and coaching the other three sales reps to do better, too. He continued to impress everyone and Dale appreciated that his competitiveness and ambition were important drivers for sales success, even if his ego sometimes got in the way of a cooperative team effort.

When they were all seated, Dale presented the question of the day.

"How are we going to position the 2400 Series of EXL monitors in our current product mix?"

The 2400 Series were new models of EXL monitors, two 14" displays, one 15" and one 17", manufactured by KCS that competed directly, model by model, with the 1400 Series from Chung-Wai.

Dale's strategy for growth was to maintain two qualified manufacturers to ensure both security and flexibility of supply. That requirement, however, added to the marketing challenge of integrating the different models from each manufacturer into a coherent EXL product line.

"Guy, we already have the 1400 Series from Chung-Wai for the same four monitors. How can we market this series as being any different?" asked Dale.

Guy had prepared a comparison of the two product lines and pushed printed copies of his analysis across the table to Dale and Patrick.

"Each 2400 Series model meets all the industry standards for VGA monitors," he said. "The quality and reliability should be good and KCS may have slightly better performance than the Chung-Wai models. They're the same on almost every technical spec, except bandwidth, which is slightly better on the KCS 2400 series."

"On every model?" asked Dale.

"What does that mean to somebody staring at a screen all day?" asked Patrick.

"Yes," Guy said to Dale, "every model."

Then he explained to Patrick what he plainly thought Patrick should already know, as the Sales Manager for a company specializing in computer display products.

"The bandwidth is a measure of the signal strength in Megahertz and the higher the bandwidth the sharper the image, regardless of the dot pitch or the number of pixels displayed," he said. "Some users might be aware of less eye-strain after hours of looking at the screen, but the actual difference is probably not noticeable to most users."

"Unless they compare and see the higher numbers on the 2400 spec sheets," said Dale. "Maybe we should position the 2400 models as premium product and price them above the 1400 series equivalent models."

"It doesn't really look premium," said Patrick, gesturing to Dale's side board where the two models were placed side-by-side. "It looks kind of clunky with that thick plastic frame around the display area."

"Don't say clunky," said Dale. "Let's call it rugged. Even better, let's call it the 'Professional Series' for serious, heavy-duty users. I prefer that. I think I'll price it higher than the 1400 series and market it as our premium product."

"But the cost from KCS is lower than the 1400 series from Chung-Wai," said Guy.

"What's that got to do with it?" said Dale. "Can you sell it at a higher price, Patrick?"

"Sure, if we can persuade them it's better product. Doesn't matter what the cost is, let's just get the marketing right. I'll coach the sales reps to talk it up as the Professional Series from now on."

"Good, let's do that," said Dale, standing to end the meeting.

"Thanks, guys, I'll work up some marketing literature and a price list. The first container arrives in about three weeks, so let's sell some before they get here."

Guy and Patrick gathered up their papers and left for their offices. Dale sat down at his computer and opened a spreadsheet to start work on pricing for his newly designated, 'EXL-2400 Professional Series of Rugged, High Performance, Top Quality monitors for the most demanding users'.

He checked his watch, remembering that Jacques was coming to see him soon.

***

Dale had waited patiently at 3D Computer Products until almost six o'clock.

Now he was at his desk with Jacques, or Jonnie, Talbot sitting in front of him. The rest of the office was quiet with the lights on only at reception and down the hallway.

"You look like shit," Dale said.

Jacques had stitches above a bruised right eye and his bandaged right arm in a white triangular sling. He sat awkwardly in his chair.

"You'll look worse if you don't look after your insurance, my friend. And much worse will happen to you and your family if you bring in the cops again, asshole. I told you not to do that."

"The cops have never been here," said Dale.

"Well, my boss gets very upset just thinking you'd do that, so he asked me to call on your wife. Very pretty lady."

"Stay away from my wife, Jacques. You have no idea how crazy I'll get, if you ever go near my family again."

"Ha! You're threatening me now? And my Italian family?" Jacques grinned and continued.

"You dumb shit, you have no idea who you're dealing with here," he said. "You just need to do as you're told. Here's the deal, if you want to keep your family safe."

Dale clenched his teeth and listened. He straightened the files on the side of his desk, then picked up the cup of cold coffee and sipped it slowly.

"Nobody touches you or your family," Jacques said. He paused and looked for a reaction. "So long as you pay the new premiums of five thousand a week and stay away from the cops."

Dale swallowed some cold coffee.

"I'll think about it."

"Time for thinking about it is over. You owe me for the last two weeks, too. I'll be back tomorrow. So have it all ready, that's fifteen thousand cash. Got it? Don't screw up again or I'll be taking your wife on a date before I pick up your kids and look after them for you too."

He got up stiffly and started for the door.

"Take care of your family, Hunter."

"Wait a minute. How do I know you'll leave me alone and not be back for more?"

Jacques turned slowly and looked at Dale.

"Sorry, man, no guarantees for you now. Even if we're called Guaranteed Insurance." He smiled and limped to the front door.

Dale realized he had lost control of the situation, but he was relieved that he hadn't received a beating or worse from Jacques. He wondered what had caused his injuries. Maybe a car wreck, as he saw Jacques leave in a grey sedan, not his Dodge Ram pickup.

He headed for the reception desk cursing under his breath. He recovered the envelope and took it back to his office to add more cash for tomorrow. He had no option. And nothing to negotiate with.

How was he ever going to get these guys to leave him alone?

***

Detective Pierre Forsey was recognized by the head waiter as he stormed through the Luna Rossa restaurant and headed to the private entrance for Club Calabrese at the back. The bouncer at the door knew Forsey as a frequent visitor and assumed the Detective was here to hassle his boss, Gino Boncanno, on another incident that Forsey was investigating. Always to no effect.

"He was expecting you," said the bouncer with a grin as he opened the ornate carved wooden door.

Forsey walked into the wide hallway leading to the over-decorated elaborate Italian reception hall and dining rooms, then turned left down another hallway and stepped into a small office where a buxom Italian matron wrapped in a pink sweater looked up from her desk. She immediately buzzed him into Gino's private office.

Forsey walked into the room with its dark wood-framed panels and patterned wallpaper with heavy dark red drapes over the windows. Gino sat behind a broad desk in his wool three-piece suit, white shirt and red tie, grinning and exposing bad teeth.

"How're you doing, Pierre? Nice to see you."

"Go to hell, Gino," said Forsey. "What's going on with Dale Hunter? I thought we had a deal to leave him alone and get Jonnie Talbot out of there."

"Ah-h-h, but I had a better idea, my friend."

"Really? Let's hear it."

"Well, Hunter was not having much trouble with the three thousand a week, so I decided we should ask him for more, instead of letting him off the hook. Doesn't five thousand a week sound better to you?"

"But why is Talbot still after him?"

"Well, this guy Frank you sent me, he does good work. Jonnie is now very well-behaved and willing to work even harder for me. And he took a cut in pay."

Another big grin around bad teeth. The overhead lights illuminated the shiny brown dome of his head framed by the short-cropped fringe of white hair. He nodded at Forsey, looking pleased with himself.

"That's all good for you," said Pierre. "But maybe very bad for me. How do I explain this to Hunter, when he thought I had solved his problem?"

Boncanno shook his head slowly, letting Forsey know he was trying his patience.

"I'm sure you can explain it to him, Pierre. Maybe a dirty cop, leaking stuff to the bad guys." He smiled at his version of an explanation.

"And you can tell him, Gino gets very upset if the cops start messing in his business. Tell him it's out of your control. We've done this before, Pierre."

Forsey glanced at the two big bodyguards hovering against the wall near the back door to Gino's office and wondered if they already knew too much about his business with Gino.

"What's in it for me?" said Pierre.

"The usual ten percent."

"Wait a minute, I brought you this guy and even helped fix your problem with Jonnie. Now it may be a problem for me. How about we do fifteen percent on this one."

"I see," said Gino, feigning surprise.

"OK, you're right, my friend, I owe you on this one." He gestured to one of the twin muscle-men at the door to come to his desk.

"Vinnie here has a five-thousand dollar bonus for you. Then we can make it ten percent again, as usual. Don't want my bookkeeper to get confused."

Vinnie stepped forward and dropped a thick envelope on Gino's desk.

Forsey looked at his name on it, took a deep breath and let it out slowly.

Goddamn Gino was expecting me, alright. He pushed up out of the soft low armchair, stepped forward, took the envelope and dropped it into his overcoat breast pocket.

"All right, I'll look after my end."

He turned for the door and left.

He didn't notice Gino look back at Vinnie and give him a wink before reaching for the phone on his desk.

***

The next day, Dale was back on the phone to Forsey from his car in the parking lot outside his office.

"Listen, Pierre, I need to speak to Frank again to try and sort this out."

"What happened with Jonnie Talbot last night?"

"Well, he didn't kill me, but it's getting very expensive to keep up my insurance." *You don't give a damn anyway,* he thought. "There's nothing you or any cop can do, so please just stay out of it. I need to talk to Frank."

"You don't want to get him involved, he's more dangerous than the wise guys you've already got on your case."

"I'll be careful, but I need to speak to him."

And I don't intend to tell you more than that, thought Dale. *I'm starting to wonder if you're on my side or theirs, in this whole sorry mess.*

"I'll be in the car tomorrow morning at this number between seven and eight. I'll wait for his call."

"He may not call, but I'll let you know."

"Tell him I'll pay, if that helps."

"That always helps."

They disconnected and Dale continued wondering whether Forsey was in on this.

I need to know where Frank fits and what he can really do for me. Or maybe Frank's the problem. Maybe he screwed it up and mentioned the cops to Talbot.

Too many questions. And too many questionable players in this dangerous and expensive game that he was caught up in.

He went back into the office.

He needed another coffee.

***

Marie was sitting at reception with her back to Dale as he carefully placed a mug of coffee on her desk with a handful of sugar packets and two small containers of cream beside it.

"Sorry about yesterday, Marie," he said. "Cream and sugar, right?"

Marie turned and looked up at him, then at the coffee. She smiled.

"Something you should do more often, Dale."

"What? Lose my cool and bitch at you like an angry child?"

"No, bring me my coffee."

"Don't get used to it," he said and went back to his office.

11.

It was before eight in the morning and the rising sun reflected off the flat-roofed industrial buildings to the east. Dale was sitting in his car outside the office, looking at financial reports and waiting for Frank's call.

Sales results for March were up from last year, which he needed to keep the cash flowing, but profit margins were declining. Price cutting had been necessary to respond to aggressive new low-cost competitors and it showed in the margins. He was thinking he might raise prices slightly and blame the rising U.S. dollar exchange rate again, but customers were very price sensitive and it was getting more difficult to support his premium product pricing strategy.

His phone rang. It was ten after eight. He picked up and recognized Frank's voice.

"I hear you want to talk to me again."

"That's right, but we need to meet face-to-face for this conversation."

"Why is that necessary?"

"I have a few questions, then I may have a proposition for you. But I need to know you better than a voice on the phone."

"I prefer to stay anonymous. What's your proposition?"

Dale could hear traffic in the background.

"Are you in your car?" he asked.

"Yeah. You think you're the only dude with a car phone? I come fully equipped, man. That's why I'm so expensive."

Jesus, he's negotiating the price already, thought Dale. He paused to make him wait.

"Well, we have some unfinished business. I don't know who paid you last time or what it cost them, but I'm thinking it's worth twenty grand to me if you can solve my problem with Jacques, once and for all."

He paused again, then added, "So, do you want to meet me or not?"

"OK, you have my attention. Are you parked at your office?"

"Yes."

"OK, let's meet now. I'm at Bennie's truck stop on Fifty-Fifth at Cote-de-Liesse in a black Cadillac Seville, parked in the back away from the big rigs. You can meet me here in five minutes. Park at the diner and walk to my car."

Now he's giving me orders, thought Dale. *But now that I've got him interested, I have to take back control.*

"I've got to drop some stuff at the office first. Give me twenty minutes and I'll be there."

"I'm waiting and the meter's running."

Dale was anxious to meet Frank, but he stalled, putting the paperwork neatly back into his briefcase. He got out of the car and walked slowly to the front door.

"Hi, Dale, three calls for you from yesterday," said Marie, as she handed him the message slips. "Sylvie also has a big request-for-quote on a school board order and she wants to review it with you."

"OK, sounds good, but I have to rush out for another meeting. Tell Sylvie I'll be back by ten-thirty and we can talk about her quote then."

He went into his office, removed the paperwork from his briefcase and arranged it in neat piles with the other files along the side of his desk. He set the briefcase on the matching credenza against the wall and stretched out in the high-backed leather chair with his fingers interlaced behind his head, feet on the shelf below the window and gazed into space.

Finally, I'm going to meet this mysterious Frank the Fixer, but how do I work with him to get rid of these guys?

It feels like I'm skating on thin ice in a grey fog, trying to stick-handle around the crooks and I'm not sure who's on my side. How do I avoid getting cross-checked from behind or whacked in the head? How will I ever get back to business as usual? I hope this guy Frank has a solution and doesn't make matters worse again. My family deserves better than that.

He shifted his gaze out the window.

"OK, let's do this," he said. He pushed himself out of the chair, taking long strides down the hall he went out the front door and back to his car.

It was only five minutes away and he parked as instructed in front of Bennie's. He glanced up at the big restaurant sign above the front door and thought they'll soon have to remove the apostrophe, thanks to Quebec's new law banning English on outside signs everywhere in the province.

No more Bennie's Restaurant, now it would have to be *Restaurant chez Bennie.* Dale thought it was a crock of bullshit, causing everybody a huge waste of time and money and emotion, just to score a few political points. He found it hard to believe the Quebec Liberal government was more paranoid about protecting French than the previous separatist *Parti Québécois.* Or were they that complacent about Anglo voters not throwing them out? In a small accommodation, English would be allowed on inside signs, but only at one-third the size of the French equivalent.

Dale thought it was legislated stupidity for the whole world to see.

As an English Canadian from the West, he did not appreciate the long history of anti-English sentiment for the perceived exploitation of French-Canadians in Quebec. He thought reasonable people should just get over their old grievances and get along on the more important things in life.

The big black Caddy was hard to miss parked diagonally across two spaces at the rear of the lot. The windows were tinted too dark to see if there was anybody inside, but Dale heard the doors unlock as he approached the passenger side. He opened the door and sat in the comfortable soft black leather seat.

He was startled to see the driver was a young black man. Frank the Fixer turned his broad shoulders toward Dale and gripped his hand with a firm shake.

"Pleased to meet you in person, Mr. Hunter."

Dale tried not to look surprised and to ignore the flash of memory. Jacques Talbot had also greeted him the first time as 'Mr. Hunter'.

"Yeah, let's hope it turns out to be a pleasure," Dale said.

He thought Frank looked like a large hard-bodied version of Michael Jackson, with the same tight black curls, dark eyes and a wide friendly smile.

"I have to admit, you don't look as mean and nasty as I was told," said Dale.

Frank's dark face was suddenly less friendly and Dale noticed a deep scar along his clenched left jaw that looked like somebody had slashed at his throat and missed.

"I can be mean and nasty enough, if necessary. Depends on what you need."

Dale thought of Talbot's methods of persuasion. *These guys deserve each other.*

"I don't care about your methods, I just need you to solve my problem. Last time didn't work out so well." Dale explained. "I told you about this guy, Jacques, demanding protection money and threatening my business and my family. Forsey told me you would look after it for me, but I'm not even sure whose side Forsey's on."

He looked for a reaction from Frank. There wasn't one, so he continued.

"A couple of days ago, Jacques shows up at my house, then he comes to my office with more threats and demands more money. He looks in bad shape. Are you the one who roughed him up?"

"Let's just say we've met."

"Well, I hope you didn't make matters worse. Now he's pushing me even harder and I've had it. I need help. I hope this time you're the guy who can do something about it. I just want them to go away and leave me alone, dammit."

"Yeah, you need protection from the protectors," with a faint smile from Frank. He looked thoughtful for a moment and glanced in the rear view mirror at an eighteen-wheeler that was backing up toward his car before pulling out.

"Like I said, if you can make this go away once and for all, it's worth twenty grand to me. I'll pay that much, but only if you can make it happen."

"I may have some competing interests to sort out first," said Frank. "You made the mistake of letting too many people know you have a lot of cash to throw around. Now they're like hungry dogs who all want a piece of you."

"I know. Business was already tough enough, now I have to worry about these assholes. I just want to be left alone to try and make an honest buck, so I can look after my family. Maybe I should just give up and take a safe, boring corporate job or go back to my old home town in the Rockies."

"Could be a way out," said Frank. "Maybe you should try it."

"No way," said Dale. He lay back in the soft leather seat. He noticed Frank's phone neatly installed in the plush leather upholstery of the Caddy. It wasn't nearly as intrusive as it was in his BMW.

"I'm not letting these guys shut me down," he said. "I need to find a way for my family to be safe again, so I can get back to my business before they screw that up for me."

"Business can't be so bad. Nice BMW, mobile phone and all those computers to play with," Frank said.

"Yeah, it used to be fun. Now I'm starting to hate this place."

"There's lots of worse places to be. Montreal has been pretty good for me and I'm not going anywhere."

"Oh, yeah? So what's your story? How did you get into this messy business yourself?"

Frank looked at Dale, then sat back and looked out the windshield.

"I've been doing this for a while. Couldn't decide whether to be a cop or a crook, so I work for both sides, instead. I usually manage to keep them from killing each other." He looked amused.

"Pays all right, better then pumpin' gas or drivin' a rig." He gestured out at the truck stop.

"So, what can you do for me?" said Dale. "The police have been worse than useless and I'm not going back to Forsey again."

Frank turned serious.

"Listen Mr. Hunter," Frank started, but Dale interrupted.

"Call me Dale."

"OK, Dale. I have to tell you, you're in a bad spot and it's not going to be easy to get you out of it."

"I thought you could help. This isn't sounding so good."

"I said it won't be easy, but I'll come up with something. I have more than one friend with the police who might have some ideas. Someone we can trust is Detective Hélène Bourassa."

"You saying I can't trust Forsey?"

"No, I didn't say that. Forsey's doing his best and so am I. Hélène just might have some new ideas for us."

"What makes you think she can help?"

"Well...," said Frank, "she's a petite young lady, but very smart, very tough. She started with the MUC police in a patrol car on the streets in the east end, just a few years ago. Now she's a Detective. Too petite and too cute to be a good cop, they said, but they were wrong."

Frank knew Hélène Bourassa well. Not many people knew how well.

"We've done a few cases together. Sometimes I know the people or I have information she can't get. Sometimes I can help her with different approaches to the problem. Sometimes she has better ideas. We work well together."

"You seem to know her pretty well," said Dale.

Frank didn't reply.

Hélène Bourassa was from the working class community of Chateauguay across the St. Lawrence River from Montreal and adjacent to the Mohawk Indian Reserve of Kahnawake.

Frank knew that her father had worked for a transport company and her mother was a nurse. They both had reminded her constantly of their relative good fortune compared to the poor circumstances and hard lives of the people around them, both on and off the Reserve. Her parents had cultivated her determination to relieve the injustices that they all saw every day. Her two older brothers were less concerned with the social issues and followed the more common path of local young men into continual problems at school and frequent incidents of delinquent behavior. Hélène had seen her brothers' encounters with both good and bad police officers during their misadventures. She was determined to be one of the good cops that made a difference in people's lives.

Hélène had achieved top marks in her police technology courses at the college in Chateauguay and on graduation she was immediately recruited to join the MUC police force. They were pushing to meet new diversity goals, so her timing was good.

The work came easily to her, but the work environment presented a challenge. During the first few months, she had to straighten out some of the macho police officers before their sexual taunts and harassment got out of hand. She learned to do it without resorting to complaints to her superiors. They would have been unsympathetic, anyway. Her fellow officers soon appreciated that she was a capable and dedicated cop and a team player to be respected. In spite of her slender build and kind face, she projected an air of authority with her confident demeanor, calm words and an uncompromising glare from her bright blue eyes. She could be very convincing.

Frank continued.

"She's a real Quebecer, *une vraie Québécoise*, part French-Canadian and part Mohawk," he said.

In seven years with the department, Hélène had worked several times with Detective Pierre Forsey and he had introduced her to Frank the Fixer, whose real name she learned was Faysal Mohamed Abou.

She called him Frank, like everyone else. Within fifteen minutes of their first meeting, they had established an intuitive understanding of each other and recognized a mutual desire to oppose the wrongs they saw and could not accept. Their connection had evolved quickly and they started to spend more intimate time together, but neither one was ready to make it an official relationship.

"She's not an immigrant like you and me," said Frank.

"I'm not an immigrant, I'm from the Rockies of BC."

"Yeah, but you're an immigrant to Quebec and your ancestors were immigrants to Canada."

"Hmmm, yeah, I guess." said Dale. "And you?"

"I'm a good Somalian refugee," said Frank with another smile.

"OK, so you're a good Somalian and she's a real Quebecer and I'm an Anglo from Western Canada. How does that help us?" said Dale. "What's next?"

"Let me think about what's next," said Frank. "I'll ask around and come back to you with a plan. No worries for you and your family. Jonnie Talbot and Gino Boncanno will never know what we're up to."

"Who's Gino Boncanno?"

"Never mind. Just another gangster you don't want to meet. Unless he invites you to dinner at his very fine Italian restaurant."

Frank let another smile show, as he turned to Dale.

"I'll give you another call in a day or so. Same time, in the car. I'm sure you want to get your money's worth out of that expensive phone."

Dale got out and walked to his car thinking again that there were too many players involved and he didn't know who he could trust or who was working for who. He liked Frank's openness and his apparent independence. He seemed to be making his own decisions and loyal to no one but himself.

They say a good manager knows how to delegate.I hope I can delegate the dirty work to this guy. A guy called Frank the Fixer and his lady friend, Detective Hélène Bourassa.

12.

Hélène Bourassa looked very white and very small as she lay naked in the sculpted black arms of Frank the Fixer. They were lying in bed together in the shadowless evening light at her apartment.

"I thought we agreed not to talk shop in the few quiet moments we get together," she said to him.

"I know, but this Dale Hunter seems like a good guy. He's just trying to stick to business and take care of his family. He's taking a truckload of shit from these people and they're ready to hurt him and his family if he doesn't keep playing along."

"Well, I'm not going to go after Forsey, you know, even if he is taking a little on the side. He's basically a good cop and trying to keep the peace, best he can. We all have to make some compromises to put away the worst of the bad guys we're after."

"I know, but how do I get Hunter out of this? It's worth twenty grand for me to solve his problem. He's good for it. That's why everybody wants a piece of him."

"You do your thing, Frankie, I don't want any part of the cash changing hands."

"OK, Hélène. You don't need to remind me you're the saint and I'm the one doing deals with the devil."

"We're both just doing what we have to do, Frank. I'm not judging anybody. Your problem is getting Gino Boncanno to back off. He doesn't let go for anybody, but the real Mafia. You have any friends there?"

"Of course," said Frank.

He was thinking she might just have an idea there.

"But that's enough talk for tonight."

He lay her gently back in the bed and pulled the covers over them both as she disappeared under his muscular body. The love-making was long and passionate, but as soon as she fell asleep, Frank was back into thoughts of a solution for Dale Hunter.

Before daylight he got up and left the bedroom, careful to avoid the easel in the corner that Hélène had set up for what she called her art therapy. Splashes of color stood out in the dark. The woman's got talent, he thought.

He wondered if his sister, Mihala, had returned to her course in graphic arts at Concordia University. He was worried about her.

Mihala was sharing an apartment in the student ghetto with a rebellious young Somalian whose father was paying their rent. It was a good arrangement, but her boyfriend wasn't a good influence. She said she loved him, but they were both neglecting their studies and doing too much pot.

I hope they're not getting into more dangerous drugs, thought Frank.

He had offered to pay for another apartment, if she would get away from the boyfriend and focus on her education. She had refused.

He was meeting Mihala at her apartment for coffee as she had no classes this morning, but he knew she wouldn't be up until after nine or later. He knocked on her door at 9:30. She was up and dressed, but the bedroom door was closed so Frank assumed the boyfriend was sleeping in and did not want to be part of the conversation. That was fine with Frank. Their conversations did not always go well.

Mihala poured him a coffee and they went into the living room and sat by the window. They were on the fourth floor with a view across the street to more student apartments and above the traffic which was at a standstill on a weekday morning in rush hour.

"So, how's school, Mihala," said Frank, "getting your grades up enough to pass the year?"

"Yeah, no problem. Still lots of time before exams, anyway."

"Come on Mihala, you need to get to work and study. Passing is not enough. You need to get top marks. It'll be a lot easier then, to get a good job when you're done."

"Relax, Faysal, I'll manage. You seem to be doing all right and you never got a university degree. Lots of money and a big car, and I don't even know what you do for a living."

"Never mind what I do. I'd rather have a degree and a cushy job like you should be looking for. I don't want to have to look after you when you're unemployed and still spending too much on shit you shouldn't be doing anyway."

"It's not your problem, Faysal, you're not my father," she said. "I'm an adult too and I can take care of myself."

He didn't argue.

She knew he would continue to keep a close eye on her. He often dropped by unannounced and she only mildly objected, knowing there was no better protector than her big brother. It was Frank who had arranged to get her out of Somalia after their parents had both been killed there.

Frank had come to Canada as a seventeen year-old fleeing the civil war and tribal conflicts at home. It had taken two years for him to escape Africa and come to Canada as a refugee and another three years before Mihala was able to join him in Montreal.

Frank had survived enough conflict, power struggles and brutality in Somalia and he never wanted to return. In the process, he had lost all respect for law and order and given up on expecting any fairness or justice from anyone. He had learned to look after himself, by any means necessary.

He had settled in Montreal where there was a substantial Somalian immigrant community and he was welcomed into a group home sponsored by a local church. He couldn't avoid contact with the crime and violence in the city and he was actively recruited by some of the street gangs in the neighbourhood of Hochelaga-Maissoneuve, where he'd moved to share an apartment with three other young Somalians. The local gangs reminded him too much of the violence and tragedy that he had left behind in Africa, so he kept to himself and learned to survive on his own in Montreal.

Frank and Hélène often arranged intimate time together at her small modern apartment in a high rise tower on Ile Patton in Laval, Quebec's second largest city just across the river to the north of Montreal, or at his sprawling 1940s era second-floor apartment in the Plateau Mont Royal, near downtown. She liked to be far removed from her police jurisdiction when she was at home. Frank liked to be close to the action all the time.

13.

It was a short walk from Dale's office to the bank on Fifty-Fifth Avenue. The *Montréal Banque de Commerce* was a square two-storey building in red brick with tall aluminum framed windows topped by pale yellow stuccoed trim. Ugly and imposing, as a bank should be.

The meeting was not going well. Dale had requested an increase in the line of credit to two million and this time Rick Petrie was not accommodating him.

"It's just too soon since your last credit application to ask for another increase."

"But you can see we're growing and we need the financing." Dale argued, "We're an importer and I don't have the luxury of thirty-day terms with local suppliers. Rick, you've seen our numbers, we constantly have enough in inventory and receivables to support two million. What more do you need from me?"

"The bank is concerned that you're growing too fast and getting outside our acceptable risk profile," Rick explained.

"What the hell does that mean?"

"Well, our credit analysts assign a risk score to every account and we try to make sure that our loan portfolio stays within certain limits. Your fast growth raises the risk in the eyes of the bank. We have to reduce the lending values we assign to your inventory and receivables because we expect more bad debt as your receivables climb and more obsolescence with all those high tech products in inventory. The computer industry is notorious for those problems and we're not willing to increase our exposure to it by lending more to your business."

It sounded like a firm no.

Dale decided it was futile to negotiate any longer. The computer algorithms had decided.

He went back to the office and started reviewing his options. The old cash management mantra from MBA School came back to him, 'Collect fast and pay slow.' It was a good general principle, but real life wasn't that simple. Pressing customers to pay faster might be just enough to drive them to the competition and asking suppliers to wait for payment would likely affect both the good pricing and the fast deliveries he was getting. He didn't want to create any of those disaster scenarios.

He needed to find another source of financing for an additional half-a-million. Personally, he had nothing left to put into the business. He was already at the maximum he could support with a second mortgage, plus personal loans and guarantees.

On top of that, the money going to Jonnie Talbot and friends was becoming a strain on Dale's cash flow.

And I just offered another twenty thousand to Frank to end it once and for all. I wonder what the hell he's doing for me.

It was time for another meeting.

He made a call to the number that Frank had given him and left a message suggesting the same arrangement as last time. Frank had called back and agreed.

***

"Why don't you just keep paying the five-thousand a week," asked Frank, "It doesn't seem to be that big a deal for you. Just part of the cost of doing business these days."

They were sitting in Frank's caddy at Bennie's again.

"I can't accept that and I'm not convinced they won't keep squeezing for more until I can't handle it. I'm not going to keep busting my ass, just to pay these guys. At some point they'll shut me down and I'm trying to avoid that."

"I thought you were running a profitable business."

"It is profitable, but that doesn't mean I have unlimited cash to throw around. It takes a lot of financing to bring product in from the Far East. I have to pay in advance, then it takes a month for the product to get here and maybe another two or three months before it's sold and I get paid."

"I see. That ties up a lot of cash."

"That's right. And the more we sell, the more financing we need. We're already growing too fast for the bank to keep up. They just turned me down for a half-million dollar increase in my line of credit."

"So now what?"

"I don't know. I'm working on it. You want to loan me five-hundred thousand, Frank? I'm willing to pay above the going rate."

Dale was laughing to himself, until he noticed Frank appeared to be thinking seriously about it.

"I don't have that kind of cash, but I know somebody else who does. And they could help us solve two problems, for the price of one."

Dale shifted uncomfortably at the thought of getting more of Frank's shady friends involved. He was probably not talking about rich old men from Westmount looking for a good investment. More likely crooks with cash from criminal activity and he didn't want to know how they got their hands on that much money.

"I know a guy," said Frank and let it hang in the air unfinished. He kept the smile to himself as he watched Dale struggle with the concept.

"Wait a minute, Frank, I'm not looking to get into bed with loan sharks next. Those guys don't have a good reputation for being very flexible or forgiving, if I miss a payment."

"Dale, I'm trying to help you out here. These guys have been in the business a long time and they have a very good reputation. If you behave, they behave."

"Are you trying to make a new deal with this Gino Boncanno, you talked about?"

"No, no. Gino is minor league. I'm thinking we should replace him with major league guys. They have lots of cash and they like to move it in and out of legit businesses, occasionally. Maybe you can help them out, while they help you persuade Gino to go away."

"It still sounds like I'm going from the protection racket to a loan shark and maybe worse. Probably getting involved in money laundering. How is that an improvement?"

"Here's how it's an improvement. First off, you're right about the protection racket. Their demands will keep going up until they squeeze you dry and shut you down. Not a happy ending. But the loan arrangement is only painful for a while, then they'll want their money back to put it somewhere else and they'll leave you alone. The best part is, if these guys come in to look after you, Gino will never come near you again."

Dale crossed his arms tightly across his chest and stared out the windshield.

"I'm not convinced," he said. "Let me think about it. I need to understand how it's going to work and you need to convince me you can make it happen. Let's meet again next week. How about Wednesday? We can go to lunch somewhere."

"What, you don't like my office?" Frank spread his arms and looked around the Caddy.

"Very nice car, Frank, but let's meet again and try to work this out over lunch. There's another Bennie's on the South Shore away from this neighbourhood. It's on Taschereau Boulevard west of the Champlain Bridge on the right hand side. Let's say one-thirty, when it's not too crowded. I'll be in a booth at the back."

"All right, if you think it can wait. I'll see you then."

Dale went back to his BMW and drove it less aggressively than usual down Fifty-Fifth Avenue from Dorval through Lachine to the Lakeshore Boulevard.

He turned east, still lost in thought and driving sub-consciously he arrived at the entrance to the Lachine Canal and parked on the quay near the small white lighthouse tower with a red-domed top. He looked out over Lac St. Louis. It was not really a lake, only a widening of the St. Lawrence River between the island of Montreal and the South Shore. The wide expanse of water spread from the junction with the Ottawa River at the western end of the island until it narrowed and flowed into the leaping white water of the Lachine Rapids. The fur traders and explorers had portaged around the rapids for two hundred years until construction of the Lachine Canal.

None of this history or geography was on Dale's mind as he stared out over the lake from his car. He got out and paced along the quay.

I need to clear my head, he thought, as he stretched his arms and arched his back. *I have to come up with a better solution than trading one bunch of goddamn Mafia gangsters for another. Maybe I should just give them the keys and tell them to run the goddamn business themselves.*

***

The next Wednesday, Frank arrived at Bennie's on the South Shore at one-thirty exactly. Dale was already sitting in a booth facing the door. Frank slid onto the bench seat opposite him, after scanning the room discretely.

"So, Dale, what do you recommend for lunch?"

"I like the grilled chicken Caesar salad, no fries."

"Not big on salad, I'll go for the smoked meat and fries."

They sat quietly looking at the menu as the waitress approached. Each added a draft Molson Ex. Frank sat back and waited, so Dale started the conversation.

"Look Frank, I appreciate you may have a solution, but I don't like the idea of switching one bunch of gangsters for another. I'm still going to be on the hook with no end in sight. I think I have a better idea."

Frank looked skeptical. "What do you have in mind?"

Dale reached for the pint of beer that had been set in front of him and took a mouthful before replying.

"I'd rather not say."

Frank tilted his head at Dale.

"I thought we were working together?"

"We are, I just think you're better off not knowing too much yet. I'd like to keep you in reserve, in case this doesn't work out."

"Listen, Dale, these guys are gangsters who could get rough. You have to be careful about pissing them off. You really don't want to get in more trouble than you're already in."

"I know, I just want one chance to do this myself and try to get out of trouble, not get in deeper."

"You trying to avoid paying me the twenty grand?"

"No, no. I made the commitment and we have a deal. Just give me a week or two to decide what I need you to do."

"I hope you're buying lunch at least," Frank said. "Listen Dale, I don't expect to get paid for nothing. If I deliver what you need, then you pay me. That's all."

"Of course. That's what I'm saying too. I'd just like to try my own approach before we get you or your guys involved. If it works, I'll still owe you and we can agree on when and how."

It sounded a little vague to both of them, but they were building a level of trust that allowed them to let it go at that.

The conversation shifted and they discovered they were both Canadiens fans, unhappy with the coaching, but delighted with the aggressive personality and phenomenal goaltending of Patrick Roy.

14.

Back at the office, it had been a quiet day and Dale had just finished his rounds, checking the warehouse and the service department to see what was going on, then stopping at the sales reps' desks to find out what the customers were saying.

Nothing demanded his attention, so he settled down to review sales forecasts against the shipping schedules from Korea and Taiwan that he had received by fax that morning. He saw no need for concern about missing sales or sitting on unsold inventory. No worries, he thought, I can relax and let things work out according to plan.

Then Patrick Jensen stuck his head through the doorway.

"Dale, I think we have a problem with KCS."

"What do you mean?' said Dale.

"Take a look at this."

Patrick placed a bright orange and black product brochure in front of Dale that looked vaguely familiar. The photos and the model numbers looked like the EXL-2400 Series of monitors, but the brand name, logo and colors all appeared as KCS, not EXL.

"What the hell is this?" said Dale.

"That's exactly what the dealer in Laval said when he handed it to me," replied Patrick with disgust. "Our goddamn supplier is competing with us!"

"That makes no sense, we're their best customer in the country."

"Well, apparently they've decided they don't need us. They have reps out there telling customers that KCS is the manufacturer for EXL and they can offer the same product for less. How's that for loyalty?"

"Are you sure?"

"I am now. I've heard the rumours for a month or so, but this is the first time I've seen their literature and their price list."

He tossed a photocopy on Dale's desk of the price list he had been given by *Micro-Laval*.

"What the hell are they thinking?" Dale said, as he picked it up and looked closer. The prices would make them look very bad.

"Jesus," he said. Dale cursed his bright idea to put premium prices on the 2400 Series, maybe that's what opened the door for them.

He would have to work with his partners and threaten to cut off KCS and persuade them to stop selling their own product directly into Canada. Dale was prepared to give all the business to Chung-Wai, at least until they could introduce another supplier. Being single-sourced was never a good idea, since it just raised the risk of getting screwed again and not having any leverage to negotiate with. The annual volume for the three partners selling EXL product across Canada was now up to $30 million. That was enough to get the attention of any off-shore manufacturer looking for business.

Dale picked up the brochure and turned it over to look at the details on the back.

"What the hell! Patrick, did you see this?"

He showed Patrick the white address block that had been stamped in blue with the name, address and telephone numbers of *InfoCité* on Ste. Catherine Street.

"That goddamn Lebeau is selling our own product against us. The bloody Koh brothers at KCS never said anything about this when I was there a couple of months ago. I'll have to cancel their orders now and give everything to Chung-Wai. The bastards, how did KCS and Lebeau even find each other?"

He threw the brochure back on the table. He saw no option but to confront Lebeau and figure out how to get this stopped.

***

Dale walked into *InfoCité* looking for André Lebeau, but as he turned toward the rear of the store, he noticed his former technician, Richard Séguin, talking to a customer and pointing at the technical details on the back of a brightly colored package. Richard finished with the customer and put the box back on the shelf, then he saw Dale.

"Hey, Richard, still selling like hell, I see," said Dale.

Richard didn't look well. His face was drawn, his eyes red and unfocused and his previously fit body sagged inside his baggy *InfoCité* shirt and his blue jeans hung loosely from his hips.

"Hi Dale, good to see you," he said, with a shy smile. "Anything you're looking for? Always ready to make another sale."

"Sorry, I'm not buying anything. How's it going, Richard?"

"I'm doing alright, but it's not easy. The customers keep shopping and asking questions, but they don't buy enough for me to make any money. Kinda miss poking around inside the electronics, instead of listening to their stupid questions all day."

"I know what you mean. This business would be more fun if we didn't have to put up with the customers. But they're kind of a necessary evil. I'm sure you'll get better at it, Richard."

"I'm not so sure. It's wearing me down, twelve hours a day in the store. André keeps us going with a good supply of um, uh, refreshments, but not sure that's helping either."

"Jesus, be careful with that stuff, Richard, you don't need to get back into the booze and drugs again."

"Yeah, I know. It's OK. I can handle it, but he holds back cash to pay for the stuff, so I'm not taking home much money, either. You sure you don't need a good technician at 3D?"

"Sorry Richard, we have a new technician at 3D now. And I did warn you there would be no U-turns. Sounds like you should get out of here, though. I can recommend you, if you need me to help you find another job."

They both glanced around the store and up at the security camera to be sure this was a private conversation.

"Nah, I'll work it out here. But good to see you, Dale."

Richard turned away and went towards another customer who was staring at the products on the shelf.

Dale watched him, thinking maybe he didn't need to see Lebeau today. Then he heard his voice behind him.

"*Bonjour Dale, qu'est-ce que tu fais ici?* What are you doing here? I thought you didn't want to sell to me anymore."

"I won't be selling to you, André, and I'm going to make sure KCS cuts you off too," said Dale.

"*Humph, impossible.* Your old friend, Richard, he tells me about KCS making your monitors, so I go direct to them. They like my business and want to sell me more. And your customers like my pricing better than yours, Dale. You push too hard for low price from KCS and high price from your customers. Bad for business, *c'est dommage pour toi, mon ami.* You're screwed."

Lebeau wagged his finger at Dale, as he went on.

"You think you can stop me? You don't like how I do business? I'm going to stop you, instead, *maudit.*"

"I'm not done with you yet," said Dale.

He turned his back on Lebeau and left the store.

His mind was racing as he added up the bad bastards he had to keep from interfering with his business. Lebeau and the Koreans now, in addition to Talbot and Boncanno.

It was time for a new plan.

15.

Dale's new plan started with a note:

We need to talk.

He put it in the envelope for Tuesday with the five thousand cash and waited for a response. It came the day after the courier pickup.

Jacques Talbot caught Dale by surprise again and walked straight into his office.

"What the hell is this?" he said, throwing the note on Dale's desk.

"Like it says, we need to talk."

"You lost your right to talk," said Jacques. "We do all the talking and you just do as you're told."

"I understand," said Dale, "but I have a proposal I think will be better for all of us."

Jacques glared at him.

"OK, make it quick. It better be good or I'll make a proposal of my own."

"Right, but the thing is," Dale paused, knowing he was going to get a reaction.

"You're not the decision maker, Jacques. So I'm only making this proposal once and it has to be to your boss directly. I need you to arrange a meeting."

Jacques exploded out of his chair and leaned over the desk close enough that Dale could feel the words yelled against his face.

"You dumb piece of shit! You work with me only. My boss meets nobody, never. I have a proposal. How 'bout I break a few bones and you pay whatever we want!"

Dale felt the urge to push his chair back and gain some space. Instead, he stood up and leaned over his desk closer to Jacques.

"You don't get it, Jacques. I'm done. My business is finished if I keep paying you. You've had the last payment, unless we can make a new arrangement and I'll only make it with your boss."

Jacques' jaw set and he reached forward slowly to grab Dale with both hands, then stopped and closed his hands into hard fists, pulling his right hand back ready to smash a jab into Dale's face.

"You're pushing your luck, man. My boss does not let anybody dictate terms. You piss him off and he may just decide to hurt you more than I would. He's got nothing to lose if you can't pay, right?"

"Just let me talk to him and he'll see this is a better idea. For all of us," Dale said.

Jacques dropped his hands and straightened up in front of the desk. He glared at Dale and shrugged.

"Alright, you want to take a chance, it's your funeral. I'll get back to you real quick. Meantime, you might want to get your wife and kids out of town for a while."

Jacques turned and started to leave, as Dale replied.

"I told you before Jacques, leave my family out of this or you and your friends will regret it."

Jacques looked back at him with scorn and left.

Dale slumped in his chair wondering who was making the more useless threat, but he knew Jacques was in more familiar territory than he was.

***

Two days later, Jacques had set it up.

Dale was sitting in his car looking at the Luna Rossa Restaurant. He had never been here before and barely knew any of the computer stores in the area. It was mostly residential, just north of the district known as Little Italy. Unlike the French-Canadian neighborhoods further south along St. Laurent Boulevard where the streets were lined with red brick duplexes and winding exterior staircases, this neighborhood was all white and pastel ceramic tile on two-story duplexes with wide concrete front steps up to the double front doors. The few commercial buildings and the restaurant Luna Rossa were built in the same local style. The larger Club Calabrese rose behind the restaurant with its impressive Italian masonry and stonework.

Dale got out, stood beside his car and took a deep breath. He exhaled slowly, then crossed the street and walked into the quiet restaurant. He went over to the bartender and explained he had a meeting with Gino Boncanno.

He remembered that Frank had warned him not to mess with Boncanno and now he not only knew his name, he knew where he was. He wondered if that made it likely he would not come out of here alive.

The bartender pointed him toward the entrance to the Club where he was stopped by the bouncer and frisked for the first time in his life. Something else he never learned in MBA School.

He grunted at the rough bump to his testicles and the bouncer looked up and grinned. Dale's anxiety was bumped up a notch at the same time. The bouncer showed him down the hall and opened the door to Gino's office.

He said to the secretary, "This is the guy wants to see Gino."

He grinned at Dale to let him know he thought he must be a very stupid guy.

The secretary buzzed him in immediately. Dale opened the door and looked across the dark-panelled room to see a round, intense-looking man with a big bald head looking up from behind his desk and indicating a chair in front for Dale. No hand shake. No smile.

"Welcome to the lion's den, Mr. Hunter," said Boncanno. "I understand you have a proposition for me."

"Yes, sir," said Dale, cursing himself for overdoing the deference. *This was not a good start.*

He sat, then realized he was stuck in the awkward position of sitting in a low chair looking up at Boncanno over his imposing desk. He straightened his back and stiffened his courage. He pushed himself up out of the chair and turned away from the desk. The two bouncers beside the back door leaned forward to pounce on any wrong move.

Dale turned back toward the desk.

"Excuse me if I stand, Mr. Boncanno, it's an old habit."

He avoided saying nervous habit. He stepped forward and placed both hands on the front edge of Boncanno's desk. He saw the dark Italian features fix in a frown.

Now I have his attention, thought Dale.

"About four months ago," he said, "your man, Jacques Talbot approached me to demand protection money. Insurance, as you call it."

Boncanno looked unimpressed with Dale's version of events and shifted in his chair as he listened.

Dale continued, trying to be respectful and persuasive, not obnoxious or aggressive.

"We initially had an arrangement that I could handle at one thousand a week. I didn't like it and I really didn't like the threats that were made, but we agreed on that arrangement. Then, all of a sudden, for no reason I know of, you demanded more money. From one thousand, up to two and three thousand, now you want five thousand. That's more than I can handle any longer. We have to come up with a better arrangement."

"Mr. Hunter, I thought you were handling it quite well. But I'm a reasonable man, let's hear what you propose."

Dale stood back and looked again at Boncanno.

"I'm proposing a trade, basically," he said, "You release me from my insurance plan and I give you somebody that can easily pay more than me. It's actually something Jacques suggested at one point."

"I think he was looking to add clients, not trade you in."

"Maybe, but this is a better idea."

"Better for you."

"No, better for both of us. I can't continue at this rate. You'll kill my business and then you'll have to find another client anyway. This way, I'll make it easy for you to move on and I'll try to manage without your insurance."

Jesus, I'm starting to use their language, clients and insurance, instead of victims and protection money.

Gino looked at his men across the room and pressed his fingers together in front of his vest. He turned again to Dale.

"Who is this new client you're recommending to us?"

"Do we have a deal then?"

"We'll have to check out your guy before we decide. We're quite happy with the current arrangement."

"Do we have an understanding at least? If this guy can pay you more than me and last longer, then you'll end my deal. I'll even pay the next three weeks in advance, that's fifteen thousand as a final payment, if you let me off."

"It's an interesting proposal, Mr. Hunter," said Gino as he put his fingers together again, pushed his lips out and squinted at Dale. "Who is this guy you're speaking about?"

Dale thought, *shit, there's no going back now. I have to give him something and hope he gives me a break, even if I don't trust the bastard.*

"OK, I'm going to accept your word as a gentleman. The guy you should check out, who can pay you more and much easier than me, is André Lebeau. He has a computer business called *InfoCité* on Ste. Catherine Street East, near St. Laurent. He lives upstairs and he works with a lot of cash."

It was more than he had intended to say, but he was trying hard to sell himself out of this jam.

Gino showed no reaction as he glanced at his henchmen who also held their emotionless expressions.

"An interesting idea, Mr. Hunter." Gino nodded slowly. "I tell you what. We'll check on this guy and decide what to do. Vito will show you out."

He waved Dale toward the door.

"Jacques will be in touch in a few days."

That's it, we're done, thought Dale, as he left and walked out through the restaurant.

He was not hopeful, but he was pleased it hadn't gone worse. He was getting out of there alive.

16.

Dale waited for Gino's response.

It seemed like a long time. Nothing happened. He tried to carry on with business as usual, but it wasn't easy to forget all the issues at play and the high stakes for him and his family. He wondered if he had just succeeded in making more enemies and he still wasn't out of this jam.

There were finally signs of spring arriving in Montreal. The snow was all gone. Grass was showing again, although it was still dead and brown, and the warm sunshine would soon awaken the green leaves and early flowers. Maybe on the weekend he and Susan would get out and take a drive with the kids into the Eastern Townships to meet the warm weather coming north. He definitely needed the break.

***

A phone call at four in the morning is never a good thing. Dale was jolted awake and vaguely remembered at least three rings before he picked it up. It was a call he had received before in the middle of the night, so it was not an unexpected voice on the line.

"Mr. Hunter, it's Chubb Security. There's been a break-in at your office and the alarm went off at 3:57. We've called the police and they're on the way, as well as our agent, who was patrolling the area."

"OK, I'll get there right away."

"Who's that?" said Susan sleepily from the bed.

"Chubb. We've had another alarm at the office. Don't know what's up yet, but I'll have to go in and meet the cops and the security guy there."

"OK, call me when you know what's happened."

"There's nothing you can do, go back to sleep."

"OK, wake me when you're home again."

He gave her a kiss and got dressed quickly to leave.

When Dale arrived at the office, a police car and a Chubb security van with amber lights flashing were waiting in the parking lot. He introduced himself and went to the front door to let them all in.

"It looks like a smash and grab through the broken window at the corner office," said the cop.

"Shit" said Dale, "that's my office.

"Let me just be sure there's nobody still here," said the cop, "Can you turn the lights on ahead of me?"

He un-holstered his revolver and went in first.

They cautiously entered and turned on all the lights in the hallway and then went straight down to Dale's office. They looked in and saw a cement block on the carpet in front of Dale's desk surrounded by broken glass. The window was smashed wide open and someone had come in and knocked Dale's computer, monitor and keyboard on the floor behind his desk.

"I don't see anything missing," said Dale. "I'll take a closer look here while you check out the warehouse and service department."

He flicked on the lights in the short hallway leading from his office. The officer and the security guard started in that direction as Dale went back into his office to check the damage. It looked like nothing had been removed.

Then Dale noticed a sheet of paper lying on his desk blotter with a scrawl in block letters,

THE ANSWER IS NO!

What the hell? What kind of burglars are leaving me this message?

Suddenly, the office phone rang on his desk. *I guess Susan didn't go back to sleep.* He picked it up.

"Sorry Sue, there's no problem. I'll be home in a bit."

"Jesus, Dale, you left the front door unlocked and Talbot's here!"

"What!"

Then he heard Talbot's voice on the phone.

"Hunter, you shouldn't leave your family alone in the middle of the night."

"You bastard, get out of my house!"

"Sure, I'll wait for you in the driveway. But we need to chat. You've got five minutes, then I'm coming back to your wife in the bedroom. Did you get my note?"

"Get out! I'm on my way."

"Fine, I'll give you seven minutes and don't bring the police. You know that's never a good idea."

"I'm on my way. Alone."

Dale grabbed the note off his desk and jammed it in his pocket. He went into the warehouse where they had seen no signs of a robbery and Dale told the cop there was no damage in his office either and nothing appeared to be stolen, so the cop could leave. He explained he had to get home to his family.

He asked the security agent to stand by until morning, when Dale would come back to arrange to fix the window and make the offices secure again.

He drove back home dangerously fast.

It still took more than seven minutes.

***

"Mommy, what's going on? Where's Daddy?" Sean looked in from the doorway of the bedroom.

Susan went to him and hugged him tight, turning him away from Jacques.

"Who's this man?" said Sean.

"Your daddy's at the office, kid. He'll be back soon. He has a problem to fix. I'll meet him outside."

Jacques turned away and left the bedroom, went downstairs and out the front door.

"Come on, Sean," said Susan, "It's all right. Let's get you back to bed. Quietly, so we don't wake Keira."

***

Dale noticed that Jacques had a new truck, another Dodge Ram with a luxurious leather-trimmed cab, but all black this time. It was parked beside Susan's Camry in the driveway.

Dale pulled in behind the Camry and got into the cab beside Jacques. They looked at each other, but Dale said nothing.

"Now you know what's at stake for you," said Jacques. "And your family is easy to get at."

Dale sat still and said nothing. Jacques continued.

"I'm glad you had a nice meeting with Mr. Boncanno, but he didn't like your proposal at all."

Dale still said nothing.

"In fact, he's convinced you're doing better than you say and he thinks you're holding out on him. You really don't want to do that."

Dale sat still and worried about Susan and the kids in the house.

Jacques continued, emphasizing his words.

"Now listen carefully, so I don't have to come back and make your family pay for any more stupidity on your part. Here's the deal. First, Gino liked the offer of fifteen thousand, so put that in the envelope with your next payment. Second, the weekly ticker is now seventy-five hundred. Any questions?"

Dale swallowed and chewed his lip.

"No questions."

"Oh, one more thing. You wanted us to make a deal with André Lebeau, so we did. You'll give him as much product as he wants at whatever price he wants to pay. He'll call you next week."

Dale's breathing became shallow and fast.

"OK, now get out. Enjoy explaining all this to the little lady," said Jacques.

Dale got out and Jacques pulled away squealing the tires.

That brought Susan to the door. They went quickly inside and Dale gave her a tight hug.

"Sorry, Sue, this is really going too far now."

"Sean woke up," Susan said. "He saw Talbot in our bedroom."

"My God, what a nightmare," said Dale.

He took Susan's hand and led her into the family room where they sat and Dale pulled her close.

"We need to end this," he said. "I've lost control now and the police can't help us. We'll have to go back to Frank's solution. Breaking into the business and demanding cash is one thing, but now they're breaking into the house and getting too close to you and the kids."

He sat shaking his head. Susan was trembling and a tear ran down her cheek.

"We have everything at risk here, Susan, they could wreck it all for us. But I'm afraid we have to get in deeper before I can get us out. It's the only way to keep us safe."

"You're scaring me, Dale. But if Frank has a solution, then for God's sake, take it. Don't wait until it's too late."

"You're right. Frank knows these guys better than I do. We have to do whatever we can to protect ourselves. I'll let you know when it's sorted out. Meanwhile, we'll just have to play along. That means paying whatever they want and staying away from the police."

17.

Dale was back at the office wondering again how he would get out of this hole, when Frank returned his call.

"Give me a minute, I'll take it in the car. Call me there."

He got up and went out to sit in his car. As soon he settled into his seat, the car phone rang beside him and he picked it up. It was Frank.

"I hear from Forsey you still have a problem."

What the hell? How did Forsey know about it so fast?

"You want to tell me about your better idea that didn't work out?"

"We need to meet," said Dale, "but we absolutely need to keep this quiet, Frank. Just between you and me."

"Of course," said Frank, "We already agreed on that, just tell me where and when this time. Not Bennie's again, I hope."

"How about my mobile office," Dale suggested, "no time for lunch anyway."

***

They were sitting in Dale's BMW in the parking lot at Bennie's on Fifty-Fifth again. Frank's long frame filled the passenger seat.

Dale told him about his note and Talbot arranging the visit to Gino Boncanno. He told him about André Lebeau, what a crook he was and how he was causing problems for Dale. He explained the proposal he had made to Boncanno to trade himself for Lebeau.

"He's a dirty snake anyway and he can afford the cash more than I can," he said. "Even better if they squeezed him enough to put him out of business. That would have solved some more problems for me."

Frank looked astonished. He held up his hand to stop Dale saying any more.

"You dumb ass. Gino Boncanno and André Lebeau are already doing business together."

Dale threw his head back and held his forehead.

"Shit! I knew Lebeau was crooked. I just didn't know he was in bed with the gangsters coming after me."

"Dale, you should stick to the computer business and let me sort out the gangsters in your life. I know what I'm doing and you don't."

"OK, we're back to your solution," said Dale, still wondering if it was really a solution.

It felt like he had tried to dig himself out of one ugly hole and had fallen into another that was darker and deeper and now the only way out was through a dangerous tunnel full of more snakes and sharp rocks. He let out a long slow breath.

"Let's bring in your guys and see what they can do for me."

"Now you're making sense. I thought you might be ready for my plan this time, so I had a meeting and told them what you were looking for."

Frank handed Dale a business card.

"Here's the guy you should talk to."

Dale looked at the thick embossed card and read, Paulo Renaldi, Vice-President, Ottimo Financial Services.

"Who are these guys?"

"They're businessmen, just like you. They have a lot of cash they like to keep in play and they offer protection from any other dumb thugs like Boncanno that might want to bother you."

"What did you tell him?"

"I didn't give him your name yet. Just that you wanted to remove Boncanno from interfering with your business and you need about a half-million in financing. He's interested, but you're on your own to make the deal. Just don't piss him off like you did with Gino."

It still sounded to Dale like he was getting in deeper instead of getting out of this mess. He took a long look at Frank.

"So, I just call him and say Frank sent me?"

"That's it."

"Can I tell him your last name?"

Frank opened the door to climb out. He leaned back in with a smile. "Sure, Frank the Fixer."

18.

The offices of Ottimo Financial Services were located on Sherbrooke Street east of the Olympic Stadium. Dale had called and set up a meeting with Paulo Renaldi for ten in the morning. He took the elevator to the sixth floor and walked into the elegantly furnished reception area.

This is a step up from Gino's den at the Calabrese Club, maybe these guys are more reasonable businessmen.

An involuntary shiver ran down his spine and reminded him he was moving up in the ranks of the Mafia, not calling on a better bank.

The young lady at reception looked up with a bright smile and he introduced himself.

"Please have a seat, Mr. Hunter. I'll let Mr. Renaldi know you're here."

He waited and scanned the room with its terra cotta walls, large paintings of Italian landmarks, modern upholstered chairs and swirling splashes of colour in the Persian carpet that spread in front of the reception desk. He was staring at the carpet as a small dapper man in a sleek dark-blue suit came out to greet him.

"Hello, Mr. Hunter, please come into my office."

Again with the Mr. Hunter, these gangsters are all so damn polite at the start.

"It's Turkish," said Renaldi as they left the reception area.

"What?"

"The carpet, it's Turkish. According to my uncle it's better than Persian carpet because they weave it with three knots, instead of two. Been in the family for decades."

"It's beautiful," said Dale.

Renaldi's office displayed more of the elegant furnishings and they sat in comfortable armchairs with a large black coffee table between them. The receptionist came in and placed a tray on the table holding two cups of foam-covered cappuccino. Renaldi was very relaxed. Dale was not.

"Thank you for seeing me, Mr. Renaldi, I believe Frank explained my situation and told you what I'm looking for."

"Yes, I understand you are looking for additional financing of $500,000 over your current bank loans. What is your current credit limit at the bank, Mr. Hunter?"

"We're at $1.5 million."

"That's a lot of debt to carry, are you sure you have the cash flow to meet new obligations to us? If we advance you the money, we are quite strict with our clients about meeting the terms of payment."

Yeah, right, that sounds much nicer than the truth.

"Well, my business is growing fast and it's quite profitable,' Dale said. "But I still need more financing. Cash flow will be better again with increasing revenues. But, of course, it all depends on your terms."

"Of course," Renaldi said with a tight smile, "Let's look at some specifics."

"If we're comfortable with your ability to pay us back, we'll advance the full $500,000 immediately. Our fees will be ten thousand a week."

He paused to sip his hot coffee.

"You'll pay the full amount back any time we ask for it, but we expect to leave it with you for six to eight months. A very straight-forward arrangement."

Dale fingered his chin as he considered the implications, although he realized that analyzing the deal or trying to negotiate better terms was useless. Of course it was expensive, but now that he was here it was take it or leave it. Walking away from it was probably no longer an option, either. He searched for something he could counter with.

"That seems awfully expensive at ten thousand a week. And I don't like the uncertainty of having to pay it back any time, on demand. Let's agree to a minimum term of twelve months. I'll make quarterly payments to reduce the balance and you can reduce the weekly payments pro rata to the outstanding balance."

"No, that's much too complicated."

Renaldi placed his cup carefully back on the tray.

"Mr. Hunter, you're forgetting you asked us to replace your current arrangement which is costing you almost the same and does not even include any financing. We normally would be charging interest of three percent a month just on the loan. We are being very generous loaning you our surplus cash and providing protection for almost nothing."

Now the shark is here, thought Dale. He chewed his lip and reached forward to take a sip of the coffee that was untouched, sitting in front of him. It was still hot. Renaldi watched him and waited patiently.

"Can I be sure of protection from Boncanno? He won't be happy to hear I've switched my business from him to you," said Dale.

"Just be sure to let Boncanno know we are now doing business with you," said Renaldi. "He's the only one you need protection from and he'll stay away from you, if he knows we're there now."

Dale put his cup down and leaned forward across the coffee table to shake Renaldi's hand.

"OK, let's go ahead with your proposal."

Renaldi looked pleased, but not surprised. Dale expected that most of Ottimo's clients quickly realized they had no better options and accepted the terms.

"One more thing," said Renaldi. He pulled a business card out of his suit jacket pocket and pushed it across the coffee table to Dale. "Do you have a business card for me?"

Dale picked up the same thick embossed Ottimo business card he had received from Frank and pulled one of his own out of his leather Day-Timer to hand to Renaldi. He was conscious of the much thinner card stock and the pale graphics on his 3D Computer Products business card. He had designed it himself and had them printed by the local Kwik-Kopy franchise. He made a mental note to upgrade his business cards for a better impression next time.

Renaldi looked at the card and handed it back to Dale with his heavy ball-point pen.

"Would you please write your home address on the back of the card?" he said. "Also the name of your wife and kids. Just to complete our file," he added with a tight smile. "Then we can include them in the protection."

Dale hesitated and thought, *OK, also not negotiable.*

He turned his business card over and wrote on the back before handing it to Renaldi again.

"Thank you,' said Renaldi. "We'll deliver the bank draft to your office tomorrow after lunch."

Even better than a real bank. This may work out well, after all.

They shook hands and the deal was done.

19.

The next day, Patrick Jensen had asked Dale to join him for lunch and they were sitting at a red-topped Formica and chrome table in Bennie's Restaurant on Fifty-Fifth Avenue. Dale had assumed Patrick wanted to brag about a big sale he had made and was surprised to hear him start the conversation differently.

"I think we have a problem with Ken and we're going to have to do something about it."

Ken McDonald was a sales rep who had been hired about seven months earlier and reported to Patrick. Dale knew his sales results had been disappointing, but he was not aware of any other issues.

"What's the problem?"

"There's a few actually. You remember, we already had a complaint from Jean-Guy at Phoenix. Ken was spending more time hitting on the young ladies there than supporting the Phoenix sales team on our product."

"Yeah, I thought you had talked to him about that."

"I did. But it's more than that and it seems to be getting worse. I think the guy has a drug problem."

"Hey, that's serious. Why do you think that?"

The stories took a while to tell.

Apparently, Ken had a lot of bad habits that were more expensive than he could handle. He had asked Monique for a cash advance on his pay check more than once and Patrick had recently heard from a customer in Trois Rivières that he had asked him for cash, too.

"Forgot my wallet at home this morning," was Ken's excuse.

"He gave Ken two hundred dollars. But he told me he was counting on you to pay it back, if necessary, Dale," Patrick said.

"Holy shit, he's out of control. That's not the way I want customers to remember us. Didn't we check this guy out, before we hired him?"

"Yeah," said Patrick, "Don't you remember? His previous employers said he had some issues and was a challenge to manage. We decided we could handle him and his issues, because we're such good managers. But mostly, we hired him because he brought some really good customers and we thought they all loved him."

"Humph. Arrogant, stupid pricks aren't we?"

"So what do we do about him now?"

"Well, he's gotta go. Even if the customers love him. I think we'll keep them, they love us too. I'd say take him aside this afternoon, walk him to the door and take away his keys. I don't want him to do any more damage before he goes."

Patrick nodded his agreement, as Dale continued.

"Call a staff meeting tomorrow and let everybody know what happened. It's important they know what they'll get fired for, if they ever make the same mistakes. I'm a nice guy, but I'm not that forgiving for screw-ups like Ken. Make sure they all get the message not to bring their personal problems to work."

They went back to their lunch without further discussion of Ken.

"What about André Lebeau and KCS product. Any progress there?" asked Patrick.

Dale didn't look up from his plate.

"I'm working on it. Lebeau may still be a problem for a while, but I've cancelled the scheduled orders with KCS and moved them to

Chung-Wai. There's still some KCS product on the way that's already paid for, so keep on selling it. Just keep an eye on the pricing, so we don't get embarrassed by Lebeau. Let me know if we need to revise the 2400 Series pricing to get rid of the balance of stock."

As they returned from lunch and pulled into the parking lot at 3D Computers in Patrick's Impala, Dale noticed a black Lincoln Town Car parked along the curb in front of the entrance.

Who the hell is this? That's a bigger car than I'm used to seeing in our parking lot.

They walked towards the front door and as they started past the car, the dark-tinted rear window slid down and Paulo Renaldi looked out at Dale.

"I don't like to be kept waiting, Mr. Hunter. I thought we agreed to meet after lunch."

"Go ahead, Patrick," said Dale as he stopped and went to the car window.

"I thought you wanted our financing," said Renaldi. No fake friendly politeness today.

"Oh, yes sir, I do," said Dale. "But I thought you were sending a courier with the bank draft. I wasn't expecting you to come yourself. Did we forget something yesterday?"

"It's a lot of money, Mr. Hunter. I like to see where it's going and be sure that it will come back when we want it. May I come in?"

"Of course," said Dale, "I'd be pleased to show you around."

Interesting, our regular banker never made the effort to visit us. Another complaint for Petrie, if I ever get the chance.

The driver got out quickly and opened the door for Renaldi who looked very small beside his bulky protector. He was bundled tightly in a grey three-piece suit with a bright blue tie and white shirt showing at the collar and a black felt fedora sitting snugly over his shiny dyed-black hair.

The driver parked the limo as Dale and Renaldi went inside. Dale declined to introduce Renaldi to his staff and led him quickly down the hall past the sales desks into his office.

"We've been in this location for a little over two years," he said.

Renaldi had not unbuttoned his suit jacket or removed his hat. His hands were laced in front of him, lips pressed shut, as Dale rambled on.

"It's 16,000 square feet with the offices in front and two bays in the warehouse, one with a ramp and drive-in door and the other with a loading dock to receive containers and load transport trucks for outbound shipments. Rent is $4800 a month. Would you like to see the service department and warehouse?"

He looked at Renaldi nodding slowly. As they walked past the technician's benches, he continued.

"Everything we sell has a warranty against failure or defects and we usually get paid by the manufacturer to fix it or return it. For EXL monitors, it's our own brand name and the manufacturers are in Korea and Taiwan, so we fix them at our expense. To stand out against the competition and show confidence in our product, we sell them with a two-year warranty."

"That sounds risky," said Renaldi.

"If there's a recurring failure or problem, we can go back to the manufacturers to fix it and compensate us, but yeah, it can be expensive."

Rounding the corner, they stopped in the warehouse and Dale pointed out the stacks of monitor boxes on pallets neatly organized by model and the locked steel cabinets where the high-value video cards were kept.

"The highest volume product is the low-cost 14" VGA color monitor," said Dale, "The best profit margins are on the larger high resolution monitors. Maybe you'd like a new 17" screen for your office? It would be a big improvement over that old IBM I saw on your desk."

Renaldi allowed a smile.

"Why, thank you. Yes, I would like to upgrade."

Dale walked over to the dock where they were loading a customer's mini-van and spoke to the shipper.

"Pierre-Luc, can you set aside an EXL-1760 and bring me the paperwork. Thanks."

Renaldi stood still, looking at the large quantity of high technology computer products. He scanned the entire warehouse.

"What's all this stock worth?"

"We have about $1.2 million in inventory right now," said Dale.

"Let's go back to your office," Renaldi said.

What now? Surely he's not tightening the screws already? Maybe the gift will lighten him up a little.

Renaldi followed Dale to his office where the driver was already seated, waiting for them. Renaldi gestured for Dale to sit at his desk, while he remained standing.

The coat and suit jacket were now unbuttoned and Renaldi reached into his inside breast pocket. Dale swallowed hard as the hand disappeared, then reappeared holding a plain white business envelope which he placed on the desk blotter in front of Dale.

"That's a certified bank draft for five hundred thousand dollars. You should take it to your bank today."

"Thank you," said Dale. *I was expecting a briefcase full of cash like in the movies, but this is much more professional.*

"Now I want you to sign ten or twelve checks for me to cash for the weekly payments," Renaldi said. "I'll let you know when we need more."

"Oh, OK." *I guess that's reasonable*, thought Dale.

"I'll ask Monique to prepare them right away. Made out to Ottimo for $10,000 each, dated Friday of each week?"

"No. Just sign them blank and we'll fill them in ourselves. The first payment will be dated tomorrow."

That was not quite so reasonable.

"But I need to know how much and when, so I can manage the cash flow."

"Just assume it's ten thousand every week, starting tomorrow. You're putting half-a-million in the bank today to cover them, right?"

The tight smile again confirmed his terms were not negotiable.

"One more thing," said Renaldi, "Tell Gino Boncanno right away that he is done with you and must stay away. We won't tolerate any interference in our business here."

This soft spoken little man could be convincingly menacing when he needed to be.

"I understand," said Dale, "the message will be delivered with pleasure."

Renaldi left with his new 17" monitor sitting in the trunk of the Lincoln.

Dale sat staring at the envelope in front of him. He held it at the corners and moved it into the centre of his blotter where it was perfectly framed by the black leather edges.

He drummed his fingers on the envelope, then he opened it to look at the bank draft, leaned back and thought about his next move.

20.

Dale was concerned about the blank checks he had given to Renaldi, but he did find it satisfying to take the $500,000 draft and deposit it at the bank. *That takes the pressure off the line of credit. Petrie should be pleased.*

He had retrieved the envelope for Guaranteed Insurance from reception and replaced the cash with another hand-written note for Jacques.

This should get a fast reaction, hopefully not a violent one, thought Dale.

He returned to his desk, shuffled through the mail in his inbox and tossed the letters and invoices back, without opening them. He turned to his computer and opened the spreadsheet for cash flow forecasts to enter the $500,000 deposit and revise his projections. It was going to be tough to pay the ten thousand a week and then the full five hundred thousand back when they wanted it. He had to start looking for another source of financing and be prepared to repay the loan from Ottimo Finance when the time came.

He hoped it wasn't any time soon.

***

It was a Tuesday afternoon and Jacques Talbot was lounging at the bar of *Taverne Leblanc*, reading *Le Journal de Montréal* with one foot up on the stool beside him and the remains of a sandwich on the plate beside his foam-stained empty beer glass.

He heard the sound of a Harley Davidson come to a stop outside the door and his courier came in, pausing to look for Jacques in the dim interior light. The biker approached, holding out a thin envelope dangling it by one corner, as if it were about to explode.

Jacques snatched it from him and scowled, realizing immediately there was no bundle of cash in it.

He ripped it open and saw a note from Dale Hunter written on a sheet of 3D Computer Products letterhead.

It read,

We have a problem.

Then Jacques saw there was a second page stapled to it. It was a photocopy of a bank draft from Ottimo Financial Services for $500,000 made out to 3D Computer Products.

"*Tabarnac!* Fuck!"

That goddamn Hunter was nothing but problems. And Jacques would have to deliver more bad news to Gino Boncanno.

***

Dale had expected that Jacques would arrive soon after the courier left with the envelope, but it wasn't until near the end of the next day when his Dodge Ram pickup pulled up in the parking lot.

He came in and tossed the note on Dale's desk.

"What the hell is this?"

Dale kept his face expressionless.

"You've heard of Ottimo Finance? The bank draft is signed by Paulo Renaldi, maybe you know the family."

Jacques sat glaring at him and Dale continued.

"They're my new partners now and I'm afraid they refuse to share me with Mr. Boncanno. Apparently, there is some bad family history there. So he needs to be told to back off and leave me alone. You too."

"You think you're real smart, don't you," said Jacques in an unusually subdued voice.

"If I were real smart, I would've persuaded Gino just to let me off the hook and go away. But he thought he could squeeze me for more and he forced me to go elsewhere for financing. My bank wouldn't help, so I had to go to these guys. I did try to tell you to back off, but you wouldn't listen."

"You know I have to hurt you and your family now, before we leave you alone."

"No, no, no. Not now Jacques, not ever. Let me make it very clear for you and Gino Boncanno. My new deal with Renaldi includes insurance, as you call it, and you already know these guys will do serious damage to anybody that touches a paying client. They have a reputation to protect."

He watched Jacques thinking about what to do with this turn of events.

"Be sure you give that message to Gino," Dale said. "And remind him they wouldn't need much of an excuse to kick his fat ass right out of town."

That wasn't necessary, but it came out without him thinking too much about it. Jacques gave him a long look, but said no more. He got up and went out.

Dale watched him go back out to his truck. *I hope Frank got it right and I'm safe to poke the bear. He said they'd be afraid to poke me back, but it feels like I just traded the devil I know, for one I don't.*

He reached for the phone and called home. Susan didn't answer, so he left a message on the answering machine.

"Hey, Susie girl, I finally have some good news. Book a babysitter and we'll go out for dinner. I'll make reservations at *Le Vieux Village* for seven-thirty"

***

They could see the wooden dock in the fading light out the window and the lights on the other side of the Ottawa River. Dale and Susan were in the dining room at *Le Vieux Village*, a two-hundred-year-old three-story farm house that had been converted into a gourmet restaurant and boutique hotel, about thirty miles west of Montreal in the quiet residential community of Hudson.

"This is nice," said Susan, "You're finally trying to seduce me again. I had almost forgotten how romantic you can be, when you try."

She was sitting across from Dale at a small candlelit table by the window.

"I was trying to be subtle, but you know me too well. How am I doing?" Dale said.

"There's hope," she said hiding a smile behind the large leather-bound menu.

They ordered and started on the bottle of Portuguese red wine that Susan had selected. They talked about the kids and local news events, avoiding the more troubling issues that were on their minds.

The meals arrived. They clinked their glasses and started.

"Bon appétit."

They were enjoying the prime rib for Dale and duck à l'orange for Susan, when Dale turned the conversation to the other subjects.

"I know you've been wondering what's going on since I went back to Frank for a solution to our problems, so let me bring you up to date."

Susan looked at him and realized he was about to kill the romantic mood of their long overdue night out.

"After the break-in and the visit in the night, we had to something, Sue, and we decided to go back to Frank for a solution. He had already offered a way out by going to another Mafia family for protection and for financing. He thought they could persuade Boncanno to leave us alone, since I couldn't."

Susan went pale and put down her knife and fork to listen. Dale continued.

"So Frank introduced me to a guy by the name of Paulo Renaldi, who has a finance company, called Ottimo. He advanced the half-a-million we need to get out of the tight cash position in the business and he'll also look after our protection from Talbot and Boncanno. I gave that message today to Talbot and he'll take it to Boncanno."

He reached for his wine glass.

"That's where we are."

Susan had lost her appetite and pushed her plate away.

Dale cut off a large slice of roast beef and chewed it thoughtfully.

"I think the danger has passed for now," he said. "I still have some challenges to sort out before it's all behind us, but we should be safe again for a while."

He reached across the table and squeezed her hand gently.

"I'm sorry, Babe, this should never have happened. I was trying to protect you from getting involved at all and should've got it sorted out sooner. I tried the cops and that only made it worse. I tried myself and only provoked them to come after us even more. Now, I've got Frank helping with his Mafia connections and we seem to have things under control again."

He still avoided calling him Frank the Fixer with Susan and Faysal Mohamed didn't sound right, either. She had enough to digest without making it more complicated.

They finished their dinner and drove home without much more conversation. The romantic mood was long gone.

21.

It didn't take long for the bank to call after Dale deposited the $500,000 from Ottimo. Rick Petrie's assistant asked Dale to come to a meeting at the bank, as soon as possible.

Dale breezed in the next day and said hello to the assistant who showed him into Petrie's office.

Rick stepped forward from behind his desk to shake hands. He indicated a seat by the conference table in the corner and closed the door behind them. He looked uncomfortable and not yet ready to explain the reason for the meeting.

"Thanks for coming in, Dale. How's the family, everybody good?"

Dale thought, *OK, let's start with a little friendly chit-chat.*

"All good, thanks. Kids are busy with the end of winter sports. Nothing too high pressure, though. Susan does all the running around for the kids and still manages a few days at the palliative care centre. I'm too busy most of the time, but I try to get to a few games, when I can. How about you? Getting enough time to enjoy your kids?"

"Yeah, it's been a good year for skiing and we were up at the chalet a lot. Spring skiing has been great too. My daughter hates to see it ending. The boys are more interested in playing hockey and looking forward to seeing the Canadiens in the playoffs this year."

"They're looking good," said Dale, "maybe they'll have a chance with Patrick Roy in goal."

"Yeah, a great goalie makes all the difference, like the old Kenny Dryden days."

"You're right, but everything was better in the 70s," added Dale.

"Well, maybe not everything, look at all the money you're making now."

"Huh, the money's good, but never easy. I should've been a banker, now that looks like easy money."

"Ha, like you said, never as easy as it looks. And you're not making it any easier, Dale."

"What do you mean, Rick, I haven't bothered you in months and we just paid down the credit line by a lot."

He was enjoying this turn in the conversation and sat back with his arms crossed.

"Dale, I know you were in a tight spot without more financing and we let you down, but I'm not so sure we like to see you doing business with this new lender, Ottimo Finance."

"Oh, really? Well, their terms are not very good, but they did come up with everything I needed."

"You know they're not really a legitimate bank or finance company, right? And there are a few questions around the owners."

Dale wondered how far Petrie would go in admitting how much he knew of the Mafia connections. The bank had accepted the deposit and ignored the ugly details, so he probably wouldn't admit too much.

"What do you mean?"

"Dale, you know what I mean. You're too smart not to know who you're dealing with. And you know the bank can't be party to anything that smells fishy, or is even border-line illegal. You understand? We have an obligation to report to the authorities anything that we're suspicious about. It would have severe consequences for the bank, if we do nothing. I want you to assure me that the half million you deposited this week has nothing to do with any loan sharks or money laundering."

"Rick, I'm shocked you would even suggest anything like that from me!" Dale faked an exaggerated expression of outrage.

"Don't be a jerk," said Petrie. "I'm serious. I have to report on this little meeting to my superiors and we need to be reassuring, not smart ass about it."

"Oh, in that case. Of course the money is a hundred percent legit, just like it came from a real bank." He looked intently at Petrie and continued.

"Listen, Rick, I would be much happier to have the money from you, but you said no, so I had no choice. These guys offered to solve my problem. We made a deal that I can live with and they delivered."

"Alright, I accept that. But you need to help me get you away from these guys and back to the bank."

"Fine, you know I like that plan. But these guys don't let go very easily. What do you need me to do, so I can get back to financing from a real bank?"

"We need to see you continuing to report good profits and cash flow and building equity in the business. That means showing us solid security and good financial ratios. If that's all there, we can increase the credit line to what you need, but it will probably take a good year before I can persuade anybody here to take another look."

"It's going to be an interesting year," said Dale, pushing away from the conference table.

"Look Rick," he added, "I know you have your damn ratios to meet and bosses to satisfy and I appreciate your working on it for me, but it will take time for me to get the numbers where you want them."

Petrie acknowledged Dale's good intentions and told him again he wished he could have done more. They ended the meeting with more friendly small talk and a reassuring hand shake.

Dale was confident that their mutual respect and trust would get them past this eventually and back to business as usual.

22.

The Luna Rossa was a popular Italian restaurant for the residents of Montréal Nord and neighboring Saint Léonard. The locals were aware of the Mafia family connections, it added to the attraction to occasionally see a familiar face from the tabloid crime pages. There had never been a known incident of violence or criminal activity where innocent bystanders had been involved as collateral damage.

The warm sun was highlighting a few green leaves budding on the maple trees lining the boulevard outside the dining room where Gino Boncanno and André Lebeau were seated for a late lunch. They were talking business, but approaching the conversation carefully and eyeing each other like two hungry dogs circling road kill and trying to avoid sharing the meal.

Both were digging into large plates of pasta. Spaghetti bolognaise for Boncanno and seafood parmigiana for Lebeau, accompanied by large glasses of red wine. André had a white napkin tucked into his collar and spread out over his chest as he manipulated a fork in one hand and spoon in the other. Not all the red splotches were on the napkin.

Gino's beefy hands were surprisingly deft at winding the pasta into neat mouthfuls, which he devoured without leaving any remnants on himself.

They were speaking in low voices, alternating between French and English.

"This Dale Hunter, he doesn't like you much," said Gino.

Lebeau finished his mouthful, swallowed and raised his eyes from the plate.

"He hasn't done you any favors either, Gino."

Gino nodded.

"He needs to learn some respect. We cannot let him get away with this. He should be out of business by now and lying with broken bones in a dumpster somewhere."

"I'd like that. Go ahead." Lebeau agreed and continued with his lunch.

"Unfortunately, his new friends are very protective of their property." Gino replied. "They don't want me to touch him. He's their cash cow now. I hope they milk him dry, but I'm not going to wait on them to finish him off."

Lebeau thought about Boncanno's dilemma.

"If you cannot touch him, Gino, maybe I can. Not break his bones, but I'm sure I can break his business. He already made the mistake of messing with me, *et qu' ça me fais chier*, it pisses me off. *Il se prend pour un autre*. He thinks he's too smart for his own good. I want to see him get screwed, too."

Lebeau chewed slowly on a large mouthful of pasta and his mind meandered over ways to mess with 3D Computer Products and inflict pain on Dale Hunter. He had some suggestions.

"Look Gino, maybe you could arrange another break-in or a fire and make it look like he did it himself for the insurance. I can't do much myself, he won't do business with me anymore."

"That's not good enough, André, my friend. He needs to feel pain. His family too. We have to do more than take money from his business."

"Gino, I'd like to help, but I'm not your enforcer. Get Talbot to do your dirty work, if you want Hunter hurt. Or dead."

Lebeau appreciated the steady flow of stolen computer products from Boncanno, but Gino had recently added protection money to the arrangement.

"Just to keep my cop friends from looking at your inventory, André," he had said. Lebeau thought it was unnecessary and greedy of Boncanno, but Gino was in control. Lebeau was familiar with his enforcement tactics.

Gino put down his utensils and waited.

After a moment, Lebeau noticed the sudden silence and looked up with alarm to see Gino's stern face.

"André, we have a good arrangement, but you need to do what I ask. You don't want to refuse me now, do you?"

Suddenly realizing this was never intended as a friendly lunch, André also put down the fork and spoon and tried to look accommodating.

"Of course, Gino, I'll help you get revenge if that's what you want. I was just saying I'm not very good at the rough stuff. I've never beat up or killed anybody. I've never even used my little handgun."

Boncanno smiled and nodded his big bald head.

"I knew you would help. Just don't use my name when you do it. And I will continue to deliver those computer products at the prices you like so much. Maybe even better."

Boncanno wiped his mouth with the large white napkin, folded it beside his plate and sat back with his hands laced together over his full belly, a contented smile creasing his round cheeks. Was it the good lunch, or the thought of finally getting even with Dale Hunter?

"Let me tell you my plan," he said to Lebeau.

23.

In the dusk of a late summer evening, the illuminated red ATI logo at the top of their five-story office building could be seen from a mile away. It was a notable landmark in Markham on the hillsides north of Toronto for Dale to navigate to his meeting with ATI President, K.Y. Ho.

Dale had been in Toronto for two days with Don Leeman and Doug Maxwell, discussing product plans and sales forecasts for the next year's shipments.

It had been a long two days and Dale was exhausted from the meetings and the anxieties about his tight finances back in Montreal. He had managed the initial five-hundred thousand from Ottimo carefully and was trying to meet all his obligations, but the balance remaining had declined alarmingly quickly. He was running out of creative ideas to fend off suppliers like ATI.

Dale had scheduled the meeting in Markham late in the day, so he could continue from there on home to Montreal. He was not looking forward to racing down Highway 401 in the dark and competing with the tractor-trailers for a clear lane. He assumed the highway patrol had more trouble picking him up with their radar traps in the dark, but 80 miles-an-hour was never a safe speed. Worse if he was tired and sleepy before he started.

Dale had been introduced to K.Y. Ho and ATI Technologies in the Canadian pavilion at the annual COMDEX computer show in Las

Vegas in 1984. They had a lot in common as two ambitious young Canadian entrepreneurs in the rapidly developing personal computer industry.

"Hey, Dale, we should do business," K.Y. had said immediately, on their first meeting. "You do monitors and we do video cards. It's a perfect match!"

Dale agreed and they were soon doing business together. The personal connection with K.Y. kept 3D Computers well-positioned as an ATI distributor. Dale consistently had the best prices and available stock, even as ATI video cards became more and more popular and often in tight supply.

Dale would rather have driven home earlier in the daylight, but this meeting with ATI was too important. He was insistent about maintaining an impeccable credit rating with his suppliers. It was essential for favorable pricing and for allocation of stock when the product was oversold. That status was now in jeopardy with ATI. They were Dale's most important supplier, after KCS and Chung-Wai, and there were significant amounts outstanding from 3D Computers that were long overdue. Dale had received a call from the Credit Manager at ATI, Paul Tam, warning him that his current orders were on hold and would not be shipped until he paid the balance of $130,000. Then he would be put on COD, or even cash in advance, if his account exceeded the thirty-day terms after that.

Dale had asked for the meeting with K.Y. Ho to make him aware of his situation and hopefully to intervene and give him time to get out of this cash crunch.

Paul Tam had agreed to set up the meeting, knowing of the close personal connection, but he wasn't pleased to have Dale go over his head and would certainly not have helped Dale's case in explaining the situation to K.Y.

They met in K.Y.'s large modern corner office on the fifth floor with a view all the way across the city to the CN Tower on Lake Ontario. K.Y. was his usual energetic and friendly self, but he did look concerned. After an exchange of pleasantries and compliments on their rapid growth together, Dale quickly apologized for the slow payments and assured K.Y. that his problems were temporary.

K.Y. still looked concerned.

"But Dale, you have very good payment history, what's happening? Are your sales down?"

"No, not at all, in fact sales are too good, that's the problem. We're selling lots and bringing in more inventory to keep up the momentum. The problem is the bank isn't willing to increase our credit line fast enough to support our rapid growth."

"But Dale, we don't want to be your bank. I don't want you holding back on our payments and paying somebody else ahead of us. That's not the way friends treat each other."

"I know, K.Y., and I really appreciate your support. You've always been a very important supplier to us and I know you're giving us much better pricing than we can justify by our purchase volume. You have a lot of customers bigger than we are. But we go way back, and I'm battling to catch up to you ever since we got started together as two Canadians launching new businesses in this crazy computer business."

He hated to play the sympathy card, but he was desperate.

K.Y. smiled.

"Ah, yes, it all started in the Canadian pavilion at COMDEX. A lot has happened since then, Dale."

"You've done very well, K.Y. ATI video cards are probably the most popular on the planet and you keep introducing new products at an incredible rate. It's very impressive. I wish I had that kind of control over our own products. It's hard to build a business with manufacturers half way around the world who only try to imitate the major manufacturers and deliver at a lower price. They're never the leaders with new technology, like you. We have to sell our expertise and good service, since our monitors never have the best performance or the lowest price. Bundling with ATI video cards is a big advantage. We really appreciate your sticking with us."

He was groveling and starting to feel uncomfortable begging for help.

K.Y. smiled and closed the folder he had been looking at from the credit department. He tossed it on the coffee table between them.

"More tea?" he said.

"Yes please," said Dale, "it will help keep me awake on the long drive home."

"Glad to hear you're still working hard, Dale, not getting fat and lazy or spending your money on bad habits. Aside from your fast car, of course. Not spending your money on fast women, I hope?"

"No K.Y., still happily married and no interest in messing it up."

He wondered if K.Y. had any of those bad habits left over from his earlier career in Hong Kong. It might be a British colony, but it was still Chinese, with the corresponding business traditions.

"Good," said K.Y. "I trust you, Dale. If you say this will be resolved soon, I believe it. I'll tell Credit to keep shipping and you'll bring the account current by the end of the month."

Dale was hoping for more flexibility from K.Y., but at least he would have the product he needed to keep sales up for another month.

Then K.Y. added a kicker that Dale had not expected.

"There's another idea I would like to propose to you that might be even more helpful."

He poured Dale another cup of tea and refilled his own cup, as he explained.

"We're launching a new OEM line of products for distributors like you who sell components and peripheral products, especially monitors and video cards, to the PC clone-makers and system assemblers. We already ship the product to large original-equipment manufacturers, but this would extend the program to smaller local computer assemblers. The products are the same as retail, but at significantly lower pricing, because they're shipped in bulk, without all that expensive retail packaging. What do you think?"

"That's a fantastic program," said Dale, "Please sign me up."

"OK," said K.Y. with a big smile. "I'll have our sales team set it up. Same terms, though," he added, as the smile faded.

Dale's drive home was better than expected. He was wide awake and his brain was racing over how to leverage the new ATI program into his sales plans.

24.

Late the next afternoon, Dale was taking advantage of a few quiet moments in his office at the end of another hectic day to go through the pile of mail in his in-basket. Sylvie Cloutier tapped on his office door and stepped in.

"Sorry, Dale, I have André Lebeau on the line and he wants to talk to you. I offered to help, but he said he wanted to talk to you directly."

This is surprising, thought Dale. He hadn't sold anything to Lebeau at *InfoCité* since the confrontation over KCS product. Dale assumed that Lebeau had heard from Boncanno about his attempt to shift the protection demands to Lebeau and he was holding that against him too. Dale prepared himself for an earful.

"OK, I'll take it."

There was only one line flashing on hold. Dale closed the door behind Sylvie and picked it up.

"Hello, André, what's up?"

"*Bonjour, Dale.* I hope business is good. It has been a while since we have seen you and I thought we should try to do some business again."

Not bloody likely, thought Dale. Lebeau continued.

"I know you don't have monitors for me, but I understand you have good prices on ATI. How about you come here and we make some deals again. *Bonne idée, n'est-ce pas?* What do you think?"

It sounded fishy and Dale wasn't sure he wanted to be alone at Lebeau's apartment again. It would be too easy for him or Boncanno to take revenge on André's premises. Dale was not entirely confident of his protection arrangement with the Renaldis and he didn't want to take any chances.

He decided to stall, worrying about what André really had in mind. The phrase *'Réglement de comptes'* or 'settling of accounts' occurred to him. It was a term he had seen in the *Journal de Montréal* describing recent murders among the gangsters and bikers of Montreal.

"Sorry, André, but we're on allocation with ATI and I only have limited stock for current customers. I won't have any product for you for a while."

"But we could still meet and agree on my pricing for when you have the stock," said André.

"Unfortunately the pricing is also up in the air, so I would just be wasting your time. Let me get back to you in a couple of weeks."

"Oh. OK, if that's the best you can do. I'll call you back in two weeks."

Dale was happy to put him off and he didn't want Lebeau knowing he would be out of town next week for COMDEX in Las Vegas.

***

André Lebeau angrily hung up the phone in his apartment above *InfoCité* and looked up at Jacques Talbot standing beside him at the kitchen table.

"*Maudit*, I told you he was not stupid enough to walk in here again. He knows too much about me and Gino."

"*Calme-toi*. Relax, André, we don't know how much he knows," said Talbot. "And Gino wants you to take care of him anyway."

André cursed again.

"*Merde.* I told you, I'm not doing Gino's dirty work. That's your job."

He pushed the phone away and Talbot sat down across the table from him. André continued.

"You're the one who got us into all this shit in the first place, Jacques. I gave you Hunter's information from those stolen computers and you decided to go after him yourself, instead of setting him up for Gino."

"You dumb piece of shit," Talbot scowled. "Never mind how we got here. It's time to finish the job. You do what you're told or I'll do some dirty work on you."

He leaned over the table to hold eye contact with Lebeau.

"Gino told you the plan. If you don't have the balls to pull the trigger, I'll do it for you and then give you back your gun."

"It's a dumb plan. Nobody is going to believe that Hunter came here to rob me or that I killed him in self defense."

"You need to get with the plan, André. We'll work on getting him here."

Talbot leaned back and the wooden chair creaked. He put his hand on the table and tapped his finger on the fat manila envelope.

"Anyway, let's deal with the money you owe Gino. It's up to forty-five grand."

"*Quoi?* How did you get to that amount?"

"You don't listen very well, André. The last delivery you got was worth thirty-eight grand and your monthly premium for the pleasure of doing business with us is now seven thousand. Do you need a calculator?"

He smiled as Lebeau squirmed.

"*Jésus*, I thought we were partners. That's no way to treat a partner."

"We're only partners if you do your job. Now let's see your cash."

André pulled the envelope to his side of the table and glanced at the drawer under the kitchen table where he kept his gun.

One day he might have to use it.

***

Back at 3D Computer Products, Dale was at the small round conference table in his office again sitting with Sylvie Cloutier. She was describing a request-for-quote from Canacomp Computer Systems.

"It's a very good opportunity for us, Dale, and Alex says he's sure he can win it, but he wants our very best price and a promise we won't give it to anyone else."

Alex Simpson owned Canacomp, a computer retailer and assembler of IBM compatible PCs. He was one of Dale's earliest customers and had become one of the biggest and most loyal. *If you accepted that loyalty meant he'd give you one last chance to meet the best price he had ever received from anybody else,* thought Dale.

"What's he looking for?"

Sylvie looked at the fax copy of the request-for-quote she had received.

"It's for 240 systems that he'll be building to meet the customer's specifications. They're requesting a standard 14-inch VGA color monitor at .39mm dot pitch with the ATI VGA-II graphics card for each system. It's for several different schools in the *Commission scolaire de Montréal-ouest.*"

"That'd be a nice order to get. We're due for a few more school board orders this fall, but Alex seems to have a head start."

Dale was thinking a few more good orders like that would help relieve his cash flow problems.

"Yeah, he says he wants to work with us," Sylvie continued, "But he's also getting some very good quotes from the competition. I gave him his current price on both the 1439 monitor and the ATI VGA-II, but he wants you to do better."

"Right, better for him, not me."

Dale started calculating what he could do about pricing on the two products that were requested in Alex's quote.

"OK, let's give him a call and set up a meeting for tomorrow."

***

The next day after lunch, they went to Canacomp Computer Systems in an older commercial-industrial area off Decarie with a mix of car dealers, technology companies and some of Montreal's remaining clothing and furniture manufacturers. Many of the buildings had store fronts advertising "Manufacturer's Outlet – Wholesale Pricing" to attract any passing retail customers. Canacomp Computer Systems had a sign above the front entrance, '*Ordinateurs – Aux meilleurs prix*' and in smaller text 'Computers – Best Prices.'

Sylvie and Dale walked through the store, noting the comprehensive product mix including a pile of EXL monitors along the wall and a shelf full of ATI video cards. There were two customers browsing and one more at the cashier, where they asked for Alex. He came out along the hallway leading to the assembly area and warehouse in back with his usual energetic bounce and friendly greeting.

"Hey, guys, nice of you to come over and help me out on this one."

Alex was short, chubby and balding with wisps of curly light brown hair that moved like wisps of prairie grass as he walked toward them. He thrust his hairy arms from his short-sleeve red-checkered shirt to welcome them with enthusiastic two-handed handshakes.

Let the games begin, thought Dale.

They followed him back to his messy office where he pushed aside some computer parts, boxes and papers to clear his desk. Alex worked hard on projecting an image of low-cost operations to impress both his suppliers and his customers. He kept his expensive Mercedes sedan well-hidden in the parking lot at the back. Occasionally he allowed the car to be noticed to subtly convince a supplier that while he was tough on prices, they could be confident he was making enough money they didn't have to worry about getting paid.

Alex continued grumbling about the difficulties of life in the computer business with so many low-ball competitors.

Still setting us up, thought Dale.

"I'm sure some of these guys don't have the product and can't get it," said Alex. "They just put in low numbers to frustrate the few capable dealers like me, who can actually deliver."

"And you already have the best pricing from us," Dale reminded him. "We value your business, Alex, and no 3D customer gets better pricing than you."

"Well, I appreciate that, Dale, but it's not going to be enough on this one. I know the buyer pretty well and he's told me where I have to be. For 240 systems everybody is pushing pretty hard to win it."

Dale hoped the competing ATI distributors did not yet have his special deal for OEM products, but he would soon know for sure.

"Look Alex, this quote is important to us too, so I have a special proposal that I think you'll like. First, on the EXL-1439 monitor, I'll bring your cost down to $314."

"Hmmm, I was thinking $299."

"Sorry, that's the best I can do on the monitor. And you already know our product is better than that cheap shit you'll get for $299."

He saw Alex smile, but withhold comment. Dale continued.

"Now let's look at the ATI VGA-II video cards. You're selling them at $189 in the store and paying me $149, which is already pretty good margin at forty bucks a card, Alex. But I think we can do even better for you."

He paused and waited for Alex to respond.

"OK, I'm listening."

"Well, we have a unique new deal with ATI for what they call OEM product. It's meant especially for reputable high-volume clone-makers like you. ATI wants to wean you away from those low-cost imported video cards. So now we have the same ATI VGA-II product, without all the retail packaging that you throw away anyway, at a better price. Your cost goes down to $129."

Alex tried not to look too pleased or accept too quickly, but he had difficulty objecting.

"All right. That'll help. I'll put in my quote at those prices. Thanks, Dale. And thank you Sylvie, for twisting his arm for me."

Sylvie smiled, appreciating the compliment.

What a charming gentleman. One of the few customers that's still a pleasure to do business with, thought Dale.

"Oh, one more thing," said Alex, "my buyer friend at the school board needs a little incentive once in a while. Can you put in an extra monitor and card at no charge, so I can give him a little *cadeau* to keep him friendly?"

OK, maybe not an entirely honest gentleman.

Dale knew it was common for buyers to accept gifts, especially civil servants for some reason, but he hated it. There were policies against it, of course, and the buyer risked being fired and the supplier blackballed, if they were caught too far outside the guidelines, but enforcement was pretty lax and the practice usually included their superiors who consequently ignored it, if they could.

"He's your friend, Alex, not mine. So how about I give you a *cadeau* instead? If you win this quote, I'll give you one of our new 17-inch flat screen VGA monitors at cost or better."

"With the latest hi-res graphics card from ATI?"

"You want it gift wrapped too?"

Dale had to smile as he recognized Alex using the same negotiating tactics that he did. Essentially, never quit trying to improve on the deal.

"Win the damn quote and I'll include the card and buy you lunch, too. Is that good enough yet, Alex?"

"Done deal," Alex laughed.

They got up to shake hands all around, then Dale and Sylvie drove back to the office.

25.

It was Dale's favorite time of year in Montreal. The brilliant fall colors of the maple and birch in shades of red, orange and yellow against clear blue skies. The crisp cool weather would be perfect for a day in the country or just wandering the tree-lined streets and parks around the city. Dale could see the bright blue sky, but not many signs of the fall colors in the industrial park as he scanned the view through the office windows.

Business was good and sales were still rising, but Dale wasn't feeling entirely free of the threats from Boncanno or his henchmen. He hadn't seen any sign of them since the new arrangements had been made with Renaldi, but Lebeau's recent phone call had him worrying again.

The weekly cash flow to Ottimo was also weighing on Dale and he recognized that he had substantially drawn down the original five-hundred thousand just to keep up and meet his other obligations.

Rick Petrie at the bank had offered no new ideas on how to replace Ottimo with something more legitimate and less costly. It would be a welcome day when Dale could get back to paying for insurance that was really insurance and financing that was really financing. He didn't see it happening any time soon.

Then the ground rules changed again. It was Paulo Renaldi's secretary who called, requesting that Dale come to Ottimo for a meeting.

"Is there a problem?" asked Dale.

"I don't think so," she said, "Mr. Renaldi said he wanted to meet you to review your file with him."

Dale thought, *OK, this doesn't sound good, but maybe it's just a friendly update.*

He suggested a meeting the week after next, when he was back from COMDEX.

"Mr. Renaldi would prefer it was before the end of the week."

Not that friendly. So they agreed on Friday morning.

***

Dale arrived early as usual and sat in the elegant reception area a second time. He looked closely at the carpet trying to appreciate the Turkish workmanship.

Paolo Renaldi was just as gracious as he had been on their first meeting and invited Dale to be seated again in the comfortable soft chair across the broad coffee table from him. Soft and comfortable, it still felt like the hot seat.

Renaldi offered Dale coffee.

"Yes, please, your cappuccino is very good."

Renaldi called his secretary on the intercom to ask for the cappuccino and an espresso for himself. Then he sat again on his wide soft sofa, crossed his short legs awkwardly and smiled at Dale.

"How is business these days, Mr. Hunter?"

Several blunt and inappropriate responses ricocheted inside Dale's head, but he kept them to himself.

"Always new challenges in the computer business, but we seem to manage all right, most days."

"You seem to be a very competent manager, Mr. Hunter," said Renaldi, "We will be pleased to give you a good credit reference."

The bastard has a sick sense of humour. I hope he's not passing me off to some new loan shark. Dale nodded at the compliment and waited for him to continue.

Renaldi leaned forward for the file that had been lying on the coffee table in front of him and pulled out some printed sheets.

"I have been reviewing your file," he said.

There was a light tap at his office door and it opened to his long-legged secretary holding a tray with one large cup of foam-covered cappuccino and another small china cup of steaming black espresso beside a small plate of biscotti. She kneeled to place the tray on the low table and Dale noticed her tight skirt get shorter. He focused on the tray and reached for his cappuccino.

"Thank you," Dale said to her. She nodded and left.

Renaldi ignored his cup, put the printed sheets back in the folder and tossed it onto the coffee table. It slid up against the tray. Dale carefully sipped hot coffee through the foam and looked at Renaldi over the rim of his cup.

Renaldi continued.

"Your original loan was $500,000 and you have been paying $10,000 a week, no problem. You do remember, though, we might want the money back on short notice?"

"No, we agreed to a minimum of twelve months. I still need the funds and can't pay it back until the bank agrees to increase my line of credit."

Renaldi looked faintly amused.

"Maybe I explained it badly," he said. "In any case, we want the balance paid in full now."

"What! You want the full five-hundred thousand now?" said Dale.

"Yes. We can give you until the end of the month, if you need it."

"But I can't possibly come up with five-hundred thousand that fast."

Renaldi opened his palms and shrugged.

"We have a better investment in front of us now and we want the full amount as quickly as you can arrange it."

He continued, as Dale put down his coffee cup and placed it neatly on the tray.

"If it's not paid by the end of the month, we'll be applying interest at three per cent a month. That's another $15,000 a month you'll owe us. Of course, when it's paid off you'll still want protection. We can reduce that to $10,000 a month, instead of every week. We're reasonable people, Mr. Hunter."

Renaldi sat back and crossed his arms tightly over his chest.

"You can handle that alright, can't you?"

Dale was stunned and slumped back into his chair.

I knew this was not going to end well, why I am surprised now? There's no way out. But where the hell will I find another half a million to pay him off?

"I'll have to see what I can do," he said.

He stood and an image flashed of him throwing a punch right into the smug mug of Renaldi. Instead, he reached over the coffee table and give his hand a quick shake. Another image came to him of ripping his arm off, but Dale restrained himself and walked to the door.

The tall, attractive secretary got no attention at all on his way out.

Dale got into his car on the street and dialed Frank's number before leaving the parking space. He had not spoken to Frank in a month.

"This is Frank, leave a message." Frank never picked up his phone to answer a call.

"This is Dale, call me back. I'm in the car."

Frank called him back before he got to the office.

"Hey, Dale, what have you messed up this time?"

"Don't be a smart ass. Your friends at Ottimo have suddenly decided they want their money back. Immediately. They're not threatening violence yet, but I don't know how in hell I can pay back the full $500,000 by the end of the month. Their terms are brutal. If it's not paid they'll start charging three per cent a month on top of my weekly contributions."

"I did tell you they were not a regular bank, right? And you were on your own negotiating the terms."

"Yeah, but those are not the terms we agreed on. These bastards make up their own terms and they're not negotiable. Of course, they still want protection money after it's paid."

"Pretty good business they're in, maybe we should try it."

"It doesn't sound like you have a solution for me."

"Sorry, Dale, but this is pretty much what we expected, we just didn't know when. Is your bank ready to step up yet?"

"I'll try Petrie again, but I don't think he's ready and he never does anything that fast. I'm off to Las Vegas next week for some meetings at COMDEX, it's the annual computer show there. Maybe I'll get lucky and make half a million at the tables."

"Hah! Good luck, but that may be the worst idea you've had yet."

"C'mon, Frank, all entrepreneurs are gamblers, right? I'm due for a change in my luck, maybe it'll happen in Vegas."

"I think your chances are better at the bank, but let me know when you're back. I'll see what I can do for you here in the meantime."

Dale continued to the office thinking there was one more thing he had to do before going to Vegas for a week.

26.

It was Saturday morning and Dale was back at the office. He was working on product cost revisions to adjust for the continuously fluctuating U.S. dollar and re-calculating prices for the sales reps to start using on Monday. He wanted the price lists updated before he left for COMDEX.

Working weekends had become a bad habit, but he defended it to himself and his family by quoting a very successful entrepreneur he had read about, who had explained his secret formula.

"I cheat. I work weekends."

That kind of cheating Dale could accept.

But there were good reasons not to be alone at the office on the weekend. His friend Alex had warned him.

"Be careful to lock the doors and keep the alarm system on. Alone at the office makes you a target and you don't want strangers with guns walking in on you."

Dale knew it had happened to others in his business.

But what the hell, I'm paying for protection. I wonder how that works. Do they have a list of protected businesses that they pass around among the thieves? Not bloody likely.

He had locked the door and set the alarm. Maybe he should work at home on weekends, but it was quieter here and he had better access to the computer systems and the paperwork.

He would look after his duties as husband and father later. Sean had a hockey tournament this weekend and Dale planned to attend the game at four o'clock, plus two more on Sunday if they made it to the finals. Keira would get some attention too, maybe with her homework. He smiled thinking, smart kid doesn't need much help, but she does deserve some time and attention.

Susan had planned an evening of tennis for them at the club.

It had been a bad week for her at the palliative care centre. After days and sometimes weeks of providing care and comfort to her patients there, she inevitably became personally attached and their ultimate death was always emotionally draining. This week she had lost two patients who had suffered in severe pain right until the end.

A few rounds of friendly mixed doubles, followed by a buffet dinner and cocktails would help them both to unwind. Dale was too competitive to enjoy social tennis, especially when he was in the mood to smash a few balls and blow off some steam, but he would try to behave. That was all for later.

For now he had to find a way to keep on selling like hell and generating cash. The phone rang and he thought, *Oh shit, I must be late for Sean's hockey already.*

He picked it up.

"Hi, Susan, don't worry I'm on my way in a few minutes."

"She doesn't believe you and neither do I."

It was his brother Dave, calling from Cranbrook.

"Hey, Dave, good to hear from you. How's life in the old home town?"

"All's good here. But Mom keeps reminding me you're overdue for a visit. Still the favorite son, apparently."

"Nah, you know you're the real favorite. I'm the bad boy who became a Quebec separatist, *tabarnac.*"

"Yeah, that's true. Your French swearing is getting better, by the way. I hope you're putting up a good fight against those separatist bastards. People here are still bitching about French on the Corn Flakes boxes and the signs in Banff National Park and it's been twenty years since Trudeau pushed bilingualism down our throats!"

"I know, I know. I try to explain Quebecers' legitimate complaints when I'm home, but it costs me a few friends. And relatives too, I think. Mom sure doesn't want to hear it."

"She'd still like to see you more often, maybe next summer? Anyway, I was actually calling to do business. You have those EXL computer monitors, right?

This should be interesting, thought Dale.

Dave was a forestry engineer and had a small consulting firm in Cranbrook. The two brothers didn't often talk shop, but they occasionally commiserated over the challenges of running their own businesses.

"Yup, that's what I do for a living."

"Well, we're looking at upgrading our computer systems here and putting in a new network. The local guy has given us a proposal and it's all HP, including the monitors. I wondered if you could make us a better deal with EXL monitors instead."

"I think I can arrange that. Even give you the special friends and family price, full retail."

"Hell no, I was thinking free, for all the times I have to defend you here."

"Whoa, whoa. You're such a hard ass. How many do you need?"

"Five of your best will be great. I'll fax you the quote I've got here, so you can make sure they're compatible with HP. What a good brother you are. I'll be sure to tell Mom."

Dale laughed silently. Occasionally, this business could still be fun.

***

Susan and Dale were settled together on the sofa in the family room, feeling relaxed and mellow after an evening of tennis, followed by lot of good food and red wine.

"Can I get you anything?" Dale asked.

"You trying to take advantage of my weakened condition?" said Susan.

"No," said Dale, "I'm too tired for romance tonight, anyway."

Susan looked unconvinced, but he continued.

"Before I leave for COMDEX next week, I wanted to let you know what's happening with our Mafia friends."

"That'll kill the party mood, I'm sure."

"Yeah, it's not all good news. Renaldi wants his money back. All five hundred thousand before the end of the month."

"Jesus, Dale, how are you going to arrange that?"

"Don't worry. I'm working on it and so is Frank. I'll be meeting with Don and Doug and our suppliers at COMDEX, maybe they can do something for us."

"OK, now I'll definitely have another glass of wine."

Dale went out to the kitchen and brought back an opened bottle of red wine with two glasses as Susan continued.

"I don't know how you're going to look after it, Dale. That's a lot of money to come up with. Can the bank loan you enough to get out of this?"

"Not yet. Petrie needs more time before I ask again."

"Do you want me to talk to my Dad?"

"No, Susan. Please don't say anything to your Dad. We don't want him worrying about us and I'm sure he doesn't have enough money to make a difference. I'll handle it."

Her Dad was an old hippie and he had never been interested in Dale's business or sympathetic to his challenges.

"It's always just about the money," was his usual comment.

Dale had long ago tired of hearing his harangue about greedy selfish capitalists exploiting everyone for profit.

"OK, but we just seem to be getting in deeper and closer to losing everything," said Susan.

Dale decided not to argue. He had nothing more to say. He poured two glasses of wine, handed her one and sat down with his.

"We'll get past this, Sue," he said. "It'll just take a little more time."

They both looked into their glasses of wine and sipped quietly.

After a few thoughtful sips, Dale put his glass down and stood in front of Susan. He took her glass and put it beside his, then turned to pull her up close and hugged her tightly. He took her face in both hands for a gentle kiss.

"Let's go to bed," he said and led her upstairs.

27.

The annual Computer Dealers' Exhibition, known as COMDEX, took place for one intense week that preoccupied the computer industry in Las Vegas every November. The major manufacturers, software companies, distributors, retailers and other hangers-on had gathered there every year since 1979.

It was not only the place to see everything new in the industry, but also the place to be seen, if you wanted to be known as a player at any level in the industry. Not showing up was a source of rumours that you had nothing new to show off or your business was doing so badly you couldn't afford to attend. It was an exercise in conspicuous competition.

The exhibits and presentations were spread out over a multitude of hotels and conference centers along the Vegas strip and tied up the facilities for most of the week. Dale had been visiting COMDEX every year since the early 1980s when he was still working for AES Data.

Now he went with Don Leeman and Doug Maxwell. One year they had exhibited their EXL line of monitors in the Canadian Pavilion for some early exposure of the product line. It had been a helpful start for raising awareness of the brand and their distribution business, but the passing crowds of American and international visitors were not very relevant prospects for a Canadian regional distributor. They decided in subsequent years that there was less expense and more value in visiting other exhibitors at COMDEX to find out what was new and what might be complementary to their own product lines.

Dale found it was also an opportunity to cross paths with his Canadian competitors for an exchange of lies and insults.

"Hi Dale, how's business?"

"Fantastic! How about you? I heard you're going bankrupt."

"You bastard, I heard it's you spreading those rumours."

And so on.

It was not all unfriendly.

There was a lot to be learned about new technologies and market trends. This year, they were paying particular attention to the product presentations on high-resolution flat screen monitors and new high performance video cards designed specifically for the rapidly growing computer games market. Dale didn't see a future in it, but he was happy to supply the demand, wherever it came from.

COMDEX was always an exhausting week and not as much fun as the families and employees who were left behind assumed it was.

By 1986, the conferences and exposition had expanded to cover hundreds of thousands of square feet of exhibit space and included over 10,000 exhibitors and 300,000 visitors from around the world. It should have been a good week for the hotels and casinos, but they complained that the computer geeks and engineers were boring cheapskates who never spent enough money on booze, girls or gambling. Not like the auto show or consumer electronics crowds. At COMDEX the only visitors that made it worthwhile for the casinos were the Chinese. It didn't matter whether they were from Silicon Valley, Taiwan, Hong Kong or China, they were passionate gamblers and played for big stakes. Some never made it to the computer exhibits or conferences, spending the whole week in the casinos.

Sammy Wong was one of those gamblers and it brought him to COMDEX every year. He was a frequent guest of the casinos in Macau and Kowloon too, but he preferred Las Vegas where the hotels, food, booze and girls were all better, he said. More expensive, but worth it.

Dale, Don and Doug were not interested in the gambling or the entertainment. They had their own agenda and it usually started with a breakfast meeting together to review the suppliers and products they thought would be worth investigating during the day. They also had pre-arranged meetings with Sammy Wong and the Koh brothers to follow-up on their visits to Chung-Wai and KCS earlier in the year. It was a good opportunity to meet and return some of the hospitality they had enjoyed in Taiwan and Korea. Neither supplier had ever visited Toronto or Montreal, so the Canadian partners took advantage of their time together in Las Vegas to play host.

On one occasion they had invited the Koh brothers along with Sammy Wong and his Vice President of Sales, Tommy Lee, to a surf-and-turf dinner party together, but it had been awkward and uncomfortable for everyone, so they avoided doing that a second time. They also avoided trying to compete with their hosts in Korea and Taiwan by adding more partying and lady friends to the mix. That would have been a bigger mistake.

The suppliers made their own choices in Las Vegas for entertainment and escorts. Jay Koh was trying to scale back on the partying and get more out of the exposure to competitors and customers, while his brother Danny brought his preferred girlfriend with him for the week to enjoy the shows and other attractions. Sammy was dedicated to the gambling.

At COMDEX, Dale continued to enjoy the company of Sammy Wong, but declined to socialize with the Koh brothers in Vegas. *I've never trusted them and they've proven they have no respect for us.*

He had not talked to them since the appearance of KCS product in Montreal with *InfoCité*. The partners had pushed back hard and Dale had cancelled his orders with them. Don and Doug were still trying to get the Kohs to agree they would not ship into Canada and to designate exclusive territories in the U.S. for EXL product without interference from KCS. Dale thought they were wasting their time, since KCS would not honor any commitments they made, anyway.

The Kohs were staying at the Treasure Island Hotel and Casino, but the three partners and Sammy Wong were all at Caesar's Palace. Late in the week, Dale was coming back from a day of touring the convention halls and heading across the ornate lobby filled with fake Roman statues on the way to his room before dinner.

He saw Sammy sitting alone, staring into his drink at a bar outside one of the private rooms for high rollers. He went over and sat at the stool beside him.

"Hi, Sammy, how are the cards tonight?"

Sammy looked up from his drink and refocused on Dale.

"Terrible, I'm down $140,000 on baccarat."

"Jesus, Sammy, how did you let that happen?"

"Big mistake," said Sammy, "I always walk away before I lose a $100,000. Tonight I kept getting good cards and stayed, but I still got beat every time."

"I see," said Dale. "OK, take a break, Sammy, and I'll buy you dinner. How about another big steak and lobster?"

"No thanks, Dale, I think I should go back in and see if my luck has changed."

He slid off the stool and started toward the baccarat room.

Dale looked at him and shook his head.

"Sammy, you are one crazy Chinaman."

Sammy stopped and turned toward Dale, his face spread into a wide grin and he started to laugh. He laughed harder and harder, collapsing on the bar. Dale started laughing along, without knowing what the joke was. Finally Sammy looked at Dale, and caught his breath.

"My wife says exactly the same thing," and he repeated it in Mandarin, imitating her high voice and wagging a finger like she would.

"All right," said Dale. "Then we all agree, no more baccarat tonight. Let's go to dinner."

He grabbed Sammy by the shoulders and pushed him away from the bar toward the dining room. He walked behind him, thinking, if he's that casual about throwing away $140,000, then I have a much better idea for him.

***

Dale was at breakfast the next morning at Caesar's Palace with Don Leeman and Doug Maxwell. Their jackets were off and thrown over the back of an extra chair and both men had their ties pulled loose and white shirt cuffs rolled up to the elbow. Dale had his blue cotton button-down shirt cuffs rolled back once at the wrists, no tie.

They had been at the same spot since seven-thirty, but Don was complaining that they were not getting their continuous coffee refills after two hours.

"How can these waiters ignore us for so long?" he said.

"The COMDEX crowd of computer geeks have a reputation for being cheapskates in the bars and casinos, I guess they're not big tippers either," Dale suggested.

"Still no excuse," said Doug, "they looked after us much better at the Mirage. Apparently Steve Wynne treats his employees better there and if the servers are happy, they keep the customers happy."

"Pretty good general rule," said Dale, knowing that their style of management was more like Caesar's. Both the emperor and the hotel.

He returned to their earlier conversation.

"Listen guys, I know you were happy to get your money out of 3D Computers and sell me back your shares, but I'm in a real tight spot for financing and could use some new investment from you both."

Doug was first to respond.

"Dale, you make us nervous with the risks you're taking. You're too crazy for us, man. Like that Greek god, whatever his name was, flying too high gets you close to the sun and you get your wings burned and crash to the ground."

Dale laughed.

"OK, so which am I, a crazy man or a Greek god?"

Don replied.

"You're definitely crazy, Dale, especially if you're getting money from the people I think you are. How much do you need to get away from them?"

"About half a million."

Don shook his head.

"Jesus, you're completely nuts. There's no way we can help you with that amount."

"I didn't think so. That's why I talked to Sammy Wong last night, but I wanted to give you guys a heads-up and a chance to buy in again, if you wanted."

"Be careful taking money from Sammy, he may be even worse than the Montreal Mafia for you," said Don.

"I think we understand each other," said Dale. "We talked for a long time over dinner and he told me about his own experience with the Triads in Taiwan. He's learned to live with them and keep them out of his business."

A waiter appeared at the table holding a large coffee pot and Dale pushed his empty cup toward him.

"Sammy dropped over a hundred grand on baccarat last night, so it was a good time to convince him of a better investment."

Don was shaking his head.

"You're both nuts. You should get along very well, but count us out."

Doug Maxwell nodded his agreement.

Dale let it go. He was not surprised at their refusal to put more money into his business and happy to have free rein to deal with Sammy. That meant he could work on his own pricing and terms from Chung-Wai.

Dale had made a proposal that Sammy loan him the $500,000 and receive a reasonable interest rate as well as a share of the profits on sales for Chung-Wai products. Sammy had agreed and offered to lower the product pricing, so they would have more profits to share. It gave Sammy a new way to move cash from Taiwan to North America.

Dale hoped he would not blow it all away next year at Caesar's Palace.

28.

Back in Montreal, it was a typical grey day in November with the damp scent of snow threatening to appear. Frank the Fixer was at home in his dark apartment on the Plateau Mont Royal sipping a scotch and reading a paperback, *The Bourne Identity*, when he got a call from Pierre Forsey.

They hadn't spoken for a while and Frank was ready for another assignment, but he was surprised at the message that Pierre had for him.

"Gino Boncanno wants to see you."

This should be interesting, thought Frank. Could he work for Boncanno at the same time as the Renaldi family and Dale Hunter? It could get complicated. He would have to be careful not to get caught in the crossfire. The last time he worked for Gino Boncanno, it was to sort out Jacques Talbot. Maybe Jacques needed more rehabilitation.

"OK, tell him I'll see him tomorrow at the Club Calabrese, about two o'clock."

***

Frank was ushered into Gino's office at the Club Calabrese.

Boncanno immediately got up and rushed over to greet him with arms wide and a welcoming smile. He wrapped his stubby sausage fingers around Frank's hand and shook it vigorously.

"Pleased to meet you, Mr. Frank. Detective Forsey told me you would be interested to work with me again and he does not have to be involved this time."

"That's right, I'm pretty independent anyway and prefer not too many people involved. It's not good for my business," said Frank. "And how's business for you, Gino?"

"Ah-h-h, very good, thank you. Please, have a seat."

Gino hoisted himself into position behind the desk and Frank sat in the cushioned armchair in front. Gino noticed this guy was so tall that his eyes were still level with his own. And he did not flinch from Gino's direct gaze.

"Mr. Frank, I did appreciate your work looking after Jacques Talbot last spring. He's been no problem since then."

"Just doing what I was paid to do."

"I like that," said Gino. "So, I would like you to do another job for me."

"All right, what do you need?"

"Well, you may not know this, but the guy that Talbot introduced me to is Mr. Dale Hunter. He was a good paying customer for a while, but then he made a big mistake and decided to push us away. I need to teach him some respect and I would like you to take care of him for me."

"But I heard Hunter was under the protection of the Renaldis. It wouldn't be smart for me or anybody else to lay a hand on him," said Frank.

Gino was intrigued.

"You know your business, Mr. Frank. You're right. That's why anything that happens to Mr. Hunter has to look like an accident. I remember you are very good at arranging an accident."

Frank replied quickly.

"Sorry, Gino, I'm already doing some work with the Renaldis, so I can't take this on. They wouldn't be pleased if they ever found out I was involved. You should be very careful, too. They'll know you're behind it if any accident happens to Hunter, whatever you arrange."

Gino sagged in his chair.

"Oh. Of course." He suddenly looked concerned.

"I didn't realize you also worked for the Renaldi family. I thought you were working for Pierre Forsey." Gino paused. "I trust our conversation is strictly between us."

"Of course," Frank said, enjoying Gino's sudden discomfort. "Every client's business is confidential. Nobody knows what I know."

Gino was only slightly reassured.

"I'm sure that's the best way for you to survive in the no-man's land where you work." He wanted Frank to know that he too could be dangerous, but it appeared to have no effect.

Frank nodded and stood to leave. Gino spoke again.

"Thank you for reminding me of the Renaldi's protection on Hunter. I will certainly not touch him, or arrange any accident. I hope he stays well."

Frank looked at him with raised eyebrows to show he believed none of it.

The door was barely closed behind him, when Gino suddenly swept his hand violently across the desk throwing papers to the floor and cursed.

"*Calice de tabarnac*!"

He looked at Vito who remained standing at the back wall.

"Get me Talbot. Now!"

Frank was back in his car thinking it was time to call on Paolo Renaldi. He smiled at the memory of Boncanno's expression when the light went on. Then he turned more serious, knowing that Boncanno had no intention of leaving Dale alone.

He made the call to Ottimo and set up a meeting there for the next evening after five o'clock.

***

At Paulo Renaldi's office, Frank had to buzz the doorbell from the exterior hallway, as the receptionist had already left.

Renaldi came to the door with a polite, "Hello Frank," and led him to his office where fresh cups of espresso and a plate of biscotti were waiting for them. The coffee was still steaming.

Frank settled himself comfortably on the big sofa as Renaldi perched on the edge of his armchair and leaned forward to expedite the conversation. He did not like to be at work after five.

"Thank you for making time for me this evening," Frank said, reaching for his espresso.

"You're welcome," said Renaldi, "What's this about?"

"I wanted to talk to you about your business with Dale Hunter," Frank said.

"Yes?" said Renaldi.

"I introduced you to Hunter when he needed your services and he was already a client of mine trying to get rid of Gino Boncanno."

"Yes, I remember that. We appreciate you bringing him to us. We paid you enough, didn't we?"

"Yes, of course," said Frank. "No problem with the payment. But I have some information you might also appreciate. I recently met with Boncanno. I reminded him you had Hunter under your protection and would not take kindly to any accident he might have."

"I'm sure he already knows that and Gino is too chicken shit to bother Hunter."

"Well, he may not be quite as chicken shit as you think. Yesterday he wanted me to arrange an accident for Hunter. Of course, I said no, but I think he may still try something."

"Humph," said Renaldi, "Maybe he is even more stupid than I think."

"I warned him to stay away from Hunter, but I'm not convinced he got the message," said Frank.

"OK, let me know if he needs a stronger message. Thank you for the information."

"You're welcome." Frank took a long sip of espresso and put the cup back on the tray.

"Now, I would like to ask a small favor from you to help me look after my client."

"I see," said Renaldi, surprised.

Frank leaned forward towards Renaldi, who sat back to keep his distance. Frank continued.

"I understand you have a better place for your money and would like Hunter to pay it back very soon."

"That's right."

"Well, I would like to ask you to give him a little more time to pay it back."

"Why would we do that?"

"He's a very bright guy and I'm sure he'll find the money to pay you back as soon as possible, but he'll need more than a month."

"We can give him a little more time, but the interest will go up by three per cent a month."

"That's the other thing, can you keep the payments the same until he's able to pay you back? After that, he will continue to pay for protection, so you'll still be making money off him."

Renaldi crossed his arms and looked unreceptive.

"We don't do business that way. We're not a normal bank. Why are you so concerned about this guy?"

"I know you're not a normal bank and so does Hunter. I know you have a reputation to protect and you don't normally negotiate terms. This is strictly between us."

Frank reached for the espresso and took another slow sip before putting the cup down again.

"Mr. Renaldi, I am sure you can understand that I have a reputation too and it is important for me to look after Hunter. He is a good client and he could give me more business from his friends. Maybe more business for you, too."

Renaldi looked at Frank for a long moment, then he uncrossed his arms and took a small sip of his coffee, before responding.

"OK, we'll give him another month and then increase the payments by five thousand a week after that, until it he pays it all back." He placed both cups on the tray and slid it aside.

"Now you owe me, Frank," said Renaldi. "I'll be calling on you soon."

Frank nodded, stood to shake hands and left.

Renaldi checked his watch to see if his secretary might still be at the cocktail lounge around the corner below Sherbrooke Street. He grabbed his suit jacket off the coat rack beside the door, left his office to set the alarm and quickly headed to the elevators.

***

The plan to end it all started with another lunch meeting at Bennie's restaurant on Taschereau Boulevard.

"I'm giving Bennie's a second chance," Frank said as he slid into the narrow red-leather bench seat opposite Dale. "But you really have to start taking me to some better restaurants, Dale."

Dale reached up to shake his hand.

"But this is one of the few restaurants I can still afford, Frank, until you get me out of the jaws of these bloody loan sharks you introduced me to."

"I actually have some good news for you on that subject."

Frank let Dale wait and wonder as he picked up the menu and sipped from his glass of water on the tabletop. The waitress approached their table and Frank looked at her with a big smile.

"Same as last time."

"Me too," Dale said.

She looked confused and embarrassed, until Dale laughed.

"Just kidding, we've never been here before. I'll have the chicken Caesar salad and he'll have the smoked-meat sandwich with fries. With two draft Molson Ex, thanks."

The waitress left, making a note on her pad, and Dale turned back to Frank.

"OK, I'm ready for some good news. What've you got?"

"Trying to help settle down your cash crisis, Dale. I went to see our friend, Paulo Renaldi at Ottimo. He's been persuaded, since we are such fine fellows, that he'll give you another month if you need it and he'll only add five thousand a week, if you don't pay it all off by then."

"Such a sweetheart."

"Who? Him or me."

Dale did not respond.

"Don't knock it," said Frank. "Most people get a broken leg just for trying to negotiate with these guys. You should appreciate all the good work I'm doing for you. How'd you do for yourself in Vegas?"

Dale brightened.

"Actually that went pretty well. My partners are not ready to risk their money with me again, but I did make a deal with the crazy Chinaman who's our supplier from Taiwan. He was losing so much at the tables in Vegas, it was easy to persuade him I had a better place for him to throw his money. He's putting up a half million. Just chump change to him."

"Hey, attaboy Dale. See how well we work together when you look after business and I look after the bad guys?"

"Yeah, I prefer my business partners over the bandits you've been introducing me to. And I'm not sure the bad guys are done with me yet. André Lebeau is making me nervous. He wants to set up a meeting."

"Well, maybe we should set it up and sort things out with them," said Frank. "Gino is never going to be satisfied until he takes another shot at you. If we arrange a showdown, that'll give him the chance. We just have to make sure he misses, then let Renaldi know he tried and they'll finish him off for us."

"Jesus, now you're coming up with some really bad ideas. It sounds like you want me to be the bait for target practice."

"Sort of. It's what the army calls a pre-emptive strike. Attack them before they attack us. And we're going to be attacked soon, I think. They'd probably give you odds on it in Vegas."

"We, meaning me."

"Yeah," said Frank,

"I didn't tell you yet, Dale, but Gino is very determined to take revenge on you for getting away on him and taking protection from the Renaldis. I think he might use André Lebeau to get at you, so he won't be blamed for it. Lebeau isn't your friend either."

"Shit, I told my wife we were safe from those guys because of the protection from Renaldi."

"That's the way it should work, but Boncanno has such a hard-on for you, he's willing to take his chances. He even asked me to look after you for him."

"What!"

"Look Dale, a lot of people want to use my services, so treat me nice."

He laughed at Dale's look of disgust, before he continued.

"I normally work for whoever is the highest bidder, but I do have some self-respect. I choose who I do business with. So relax, you're still number one, more or less. Even though Gino has a better restaurant than this one."

"I'm such a lucky guy."

"Luck has nothing to do with it. But let's get back to the plan. It's the only way I can see to get them off your case and let you get back to your business. Then I can get back to my other clients, too. They're a lot less trouble than you, Dale."

"Wait a minute, I'm not sure we're done yet."

"If I can keep you alive another month, I think I deserve a bonus."

"I thought you offered a lifetime guarantee. You telling me my lifetime is getting shorter?"

"Nope, I'm just trying to make sure we don't get caught by surprise. If I can help you get rid of these guys, though, I may be looking for work. You still need a salesman at 3D?"

"That's another bad idea. I thought we just agreed I should keep to the computer business and you should keep to the crime business. Let's stop mixing them up."

This banter would be more amusing, if we weren't talking about me staying alive while a bunch of gangsters compete over how to do me in.

"OK Frank, let's get serious here. How do we set it up to get rid of these guys? I'm really getting fed up with all this bullshit, trying to avoid the crooks doing violence to me and my family."

"Dale, you worry too much. You think your life is rough here in Montreal, you should try Mogadishu."

"Where?"

"Somalia. Try doing business there, and you'll really know how good you have it here."

"No thanks."

"It's a great training ground for learning how to battle people a lot worse than these local gangsters. See this?" He pointed at the scar on his jawline.

"The gangs back home don't hesitate to hack away. I'm lucky to still be in one piece. Montreal is easy street compared to the murder and mayhem back there."

"OK, I'll let you deal with these assholes and figure out the best tactics. Somalia style works for me, hack away if you need to."

"Fine," said Frank, "but the next move is up to you. Let's figure out how we get them to come to us."

They talked quietly of their options and a plan to force the threats to a conclusion. There were several long pauses as they both reflected on the risks and the possible consequences.

After Frank left, Dale asked for another coffee refill and a piece of carrot cake. A little self-indulgence would help him relax and get his thoughts organized for their next move.

He reached for the *Journal de Montréal* that was lying on a neighboring table and checked the front page headlines and photos that were all crime stories or hockey news. The world news was relegated to page fifteen where the columnists were analyzing another failed Summit meeting between President Reagan and Chairman Gorbachev. Apparently Reagan was insisting on developing his satellite defense program against inter-continental ballistic missiles, while the Russians were arguing for a disarmament treaty. Dale thought about his own situation.

Hope for agreement on any terms for peaceful coexistence between those two is probably no better than it is for me, in my own war games.

29.

After the deal-making in Las Vegas, Dale had invited Sammy to visit him in Montreal. He was due to arrive on an afternoon flight after visiting Don Leeman and Doug Maxwell in Toronto. Dale was waiting in the arrivals area at Dorval International airport and saw Sammy coming through the crowd of passengers with his Sales Manager, Tommy Lee, pushing their baggage cart from the Air Canada carrousel.

He caught their attention and Sammy reached out with an enthusiastic handshake.

"Dale, it's a pleasure to finally get to Montreal. It's a lot smaller than Toronto, and it's an island!"

The comparison to bigger and more prosperous Toronto always grated. Dale chose to ignore it.

"Glad you had a good view from the air. I'll give you a better look at our beautiful city tomorrow."

They went out to the traffic lanes in front of the terminal where Patrick was waiting in his Impala. There was lots of room for four passengers, but Sammy and Tommy Lee did not travel light. Their luggage looked sufficient for them to stay a couple of weeks. After jamming two large suitcases in the trunk they were still forced to squeeze more bags in tightly around them on the passenger seats. Fortunately, it was only a ten-minute drive to the office.

"Let's stop at 3D for a quick tour," Dale said, "then we can go downtown in two cars. We've got you booked at the Queen Elizabeth Hotel. After you check in, we'll go out and enjoy the great food and night life that Montreal's famous for."

"That sounds like more fun than Toronto," said Sammy.

"Damn right," said Dale.

At the office, Sammy was impressed by Dale's modern, organized and efficient facilities, but he was more interested in the friendly and attractive young ladies.

"I see you have an eye for talent, Dale," he said with a wink.

They walked into the busy warehouse where the forklift was running back and forth from a container with pallets of monitors. They continued from the warehouse into the service department and saw stacks of product tagged for repair and open monitor cases arranged on workbenches for the technicians to work on them.

"You'll be happy to sell more Chung-Wai product," Sammy remarked, "all the KCS are coming back for repair."

"We get too many of yours back too, Sammy. We'll show you the stats tomorrow."

That evening, the four of them, Dale and Sammy, Patrick Jensen and Tommy Lee, went into Old Montreal, or *le Vieux Montréal*, as it's called on the tourist maps. They walked along the cobblestone streets from the parking lot at the Old Port past the historic old stone buildings and Dale pointed out some of the early landmarks of industry and commerce in Montreal. He explained how Canada had prospered from the fur trade for over two hundred years, primarily with beaver pelts shipped to Europe for the fashionable felt top-hats of the era.

"Then we switched to forestry and mining as primary industries, so we're still shipping all our natural resources out of the country and importing everything we need, from oranges and bananas to TVs and VCRs," explained Dale.

"You're doing a good job on computer products in Taiwan, Sammy. You're staying competitive with the Japanese and Americans. But watch out for the Chinese, they're getting better all the time and they're sending us some very interesting prices."

"Better for you to watch out," said Sammy. "I already told you, it's easy to deliver low prices, but hard to deliver good product. Go ahead with the Chinese if you really want more customer complaints and more monitors to repair."

"I know, Sammy, don't worry, we're sticking with you. Just want to be sure you're staying ahead of your competition."

They continued their business chatter over traditional Quebec cuisine at *L'Auberge St. Gabriel,* the restaurant that Dale had chosen in a restored eighteenth-century mansion with furnishings and costumes of the period adding to the ambience. After dinner, Dale planned to take his guests back to Saint Catherine Street to enjoy an upscale strip club, called *Chez Paris.* It would be a well-rounded evening of Montreal history and culture.

At *Chez Paris,* Sammy was fascinated by the glistening nearly-naked dancers on stage making slinky suggestive moves to the pounding music. He also noticed a few of the girls going to tables in the back for private performances, so Dale leaned over and explained to him the concept of a lap dance.

"For an extra twenty bucks, they'll come to the table and dance right up close over your crotch. You have to try not to come in your pants."

It did not take long for Sammy to tuck sixty dollars into G-strings for the close-up experience. It was well after midnight by the time Dale and Patrick walked them back to their hotel.

The next day, Dale gave them time to recover with a late morning pickup at the hotel. He did not have a spacious Impala or a chauffeur-driven Mercedes, but he did have his sporty BMW M3 to show-off. He drove aggressively through Montreal traffic racing west on Highway 20 criss-crossing the lanes, then taking a hard right turn up Fifty-Fifth Avenue and again into the parking lot at 3D Computers.

"I see you like this car," said Sammy, shaking his head as he got out and helped a pale Tommy Lee squeeze out of the rear seat.

The meeting in Montreal was intended for Sammy to learn about 3D Computer Products and to agree on their new working arrangements. The first $300,000 from Sammy had already been sent by wire transfer and deposited at the bank. There was another $200,000 bank draft in Tommy Lee's briefcase. Sammy asked him for it and handed it to Dale, as soon as they were seated.

"This should be enough to work with for a while, Dale. I trust you'll use it well."

"Thank you, Sammy, it's a real pleasure to do business with a gentleman like you and get rid of the dangerous Italians I've been stuck with for a while."

They were both comfortable working on a handshake with no written contract. The understanding was that the money was a loan, not a purchase of shares. Dale didn't want a new partner in his business.

Sammy had agreed to an initial three-month period with no interest, then one percent a month paid directly into his personal account in San Francisco. Sammy was also reducing the purchase price from Chung-Wai on all EXL monitors shipped to 3D Computers. It was a fair and practical arrangement that satisfied them both.

After sandwiches had been delivered and devoured at Dale's conference table, their meeting continued well into the afternoon.

They looked at the sales history and forecasts, as well as the technical reports on warranty repairs for EXL monitors manufactured by Chung-Wai. Patrick came in to boast about the sales numbers and defend his ambitious forecasts. Guy Tremblay presented the repair statistics and his analysis of the failures and noticed that neither Sammy nor Tommy Lee paid much attention. Sammy nodded his thank you to Guy, then passed the reports to Tommy who pushed them into a file in his already stuffed leather briefcase.

They were winding down at about six o'clock and Dale assumed they were looking forward to another evening on the town. He was gathering up his papers from the conference table, when Sammy opened a new subject.

"How's KCS doing with their own brand name here?" he asked.

"I think they've decided it was a mistake," Dale quickly replied.

"They really pissed us off with that move and I cancelled all their outstanding orders. You got those orders instead, Sammy. They've backed off now in Eastern Canada, I think, but think they're probably still screwing around in the West and maybe the US. Hopefully losing their ass."

Sammy smiled.

"Actually, I hear they're doing pretty well. In fact, I thought we should try it with Chung-Wai branded product. With your permission and assistance, of course, Dale."

"Oh God no, Sammy, please don't even think about it."

Dale noticed Tommy Lee shrinking from the table and Patrick looked up at him for a strong response. Sammy was not deterred.

"Now that we're partners, Dale, this would be a good way to make more money together."

"Whoa, whoa, Sammy, let's back up a bit."

Dale organised the papers in front of him into a neat pile, took a sip of cold coffee and sat back to look directly at Sammy.

"Let me remind you first that we're not partners. You're a very important supplier and now an important lender to 3D, but I am not asking you to help me run my business."

That sounded a little more aggressive than he had intended and he noticed Sammy's frown. He ignored Tommy Lee and Patrick, who were trying to stay out of the line of fire.

Dale continued, before Sammy could respond.

"Listen, Sammy, I really appreciate your support and I do want to work with you to build the business, but bringing Chung-Wai branded product into the mix here would backfire on both of us."

He paused and took another sip of cold coffee.

"We've spent almost three years now building a strong reputation for the EXL brand name, but it can be ruined in five minutes if we suddenly try to explain that it's not really our product. I don't want to hurt your feelings, but Taiwanese product will not be well received. Customers count on us to support the product line and we have spent a lot of time and effort building a strong team here in sales, customer service, and technical support. We don't want to shake their confidence in us and change any of that."

Sammy was not convinced.

"But we could reduce the price even more than the two percent we just agreed on."

"It's not all about the price," said Dale. "Listen, Sammy, I know it's tempting to sell direct and reduce the price to sell even more, but it's never that simple."

Sammy was thinking about it.

"OK, let's talk again tomorrow," he said. "Now it's time for dinner and another look at those lovely French-Canadian dancers. Maybe we can get on stage ourselves tonight."

Dale burst out laughing, happy at the change of subject.

"That's not what I meant by working together, Sammy."

***

When they were all back at the office again the next morning, Dale suggested that Patrick and Tommy Lee work together on the sales forecasts and the schedule for containers from Taiwan, while he and Sammy met separately in his office. Patrick looked concerned, but Dale gave him no opportunity to object.

Dale sat again at the conference table and doodled on the open notepad in front of him tapping his pen against the coffee cup beside it and waited for Sammy to get settled.

Sammy opened the file folder he had pulled from his briefcase and showed Dale some samples of the labelling and packaging he was planning to use for Chung-Wai product under the CHW label.

"What do you think, Dale? Looks good, hey?"

Dale was not pleased to see that Chung-Wai had simply copied all the designs from the EXL brand. *No bloody respect for trademarks*, he thought. Of course, they had all the artwork in their factory and it was easy to simply change the three letters from EXL to CHW.

Sammy continued.

"It seems to work for you, Dale. No need to re-invent the wheel, right?"

Dale knew it would be futile to lecture Sammy on the principles of branding and the added value he attained through effective marketing. He needed to persuade him to go in a different direction, not fiddle with the details of logos and product packaging. He had sketched out an idea overnight and was prepared to present it to Sammy this morning.

"Sammy," he said, "you tell me you're already selling the CHW product in California and competing with your distributors there. I think that's a mistake."

"They're not accomplishing anything for us, anyway."

"Right, well, I still think it's a mistake and I don't want you to make it here. We're selling a lot for you and confusing the market with two labels for the same product is not going to help. Let me propose something else. Something that will be better for both of us. Would you like another coffee first?"

"No, thanks." Sammy closed the folder and set it aside.

"So, what do you propose then, Dale?"

"Well, you know we're doing very well here in Canada and have coverage coast-to-coast for the EXL brand name. Remember it's mostly your product now, too. We still have lots of room to grow sales, as long as we build on our reputation and the existing brand name. It's a simple formula, but it's still hard work. And there's more competition here every month trying to steal our business. I don't want to give them a new opportunity."

Sammy didn't look convinced, so Dale continued.

"Sammy, look, I really appreciate you're willing to be my partner and I know you can add a lot more than cash to help us be successful together. I just think our efforts should be directed towards a bigger opportunity in a new market, instead of messing with this one where we're already doing very well. I think we have a much better chance of success if we work together on a joint venture in New England."

Now Sammy perked up.

"That's a good market," he said, "probably bigger than here too. We don't do any business at all in New England."

"Absolutely right. It's three times, maybe five times, the size of the market in all of Eastern Canada. I've been looking at expanding there and tested the market already with a few visits to the computer dealers in Burlington, Vermont and Plattsburg, New York. They're only a forty-five minute drive from here." he added.

Sammy was nodding appreciatively, as Dale continued.

"The dealers in New England like the product and the price, but we have the hassle of the border crossing and they keep telling me, 'We'd rather buy American product from our American neighbors,' even if their American neighbour is four hours away in Boston."

"Hmmm, this is getting very interesting," said Sammy.

"In fact," Dale said, "If you agree to stay out of Canada with CHW product and only ship it to the U.S., I think Don and Doug would also be very happy about our joint venture in Boston."

"You know, Dale, sometimes you start to make sense to me. I like this idea."

"Good," said Dale. *That's a relief, now let's get the ball rolling in the right direction before he comes back at me with any more bad ideas.*

"OK," he said, "Let's finalize our work here today, then you can send Tommy home to look after business in Taiwan and we can drive to Boston tomorrow. It's a beautiful drive through Vermont and everybody seems to ignore the speed limit. We can get moving on our plan and you can look at the space I have an option on. Ready to rock and roll in Boston, Sammy?"

Dale was concerned about being away from Montreal with all he knew from Frank about Boncanno and Talbot seeking revenge, but he needed to resolve this issue right away before Sammy gave him any more problems to deal with.

Sammy raised his coffee cup in a toast to their new plan.

"Sounds good, let's go," he said.

They called it a day and went looking for their colleagues to advise them of the change in plans.

***

The trip to Boston went better than Dale expected. They left early into the sunrise over the Champlain Bridge and south through the mountains of Quebec and Vermont where a few bare trees still had remnants of the bright fall colors. There was no snow yet and the roads were dry and bare. It took them four hours and thirty-five minutes from downtown Montreal to the Boston city limits.

They continued on to the small distribution centre that Dale had found in Norton, Massachusetts, a few miles southwest of Boston. After showing Sammy the property and making a deal on a three-year lease, they left a deposit check with the agent to hold the space for them. They agreed on a plan to open in February with initial staff and starting inventory from Montreal until they could recruit local talent and deliver more product from Taiwan.

That evening, they drove back to Boston and checked into their hotel. Sammy had already spent enough time in California to know that evenings in America were not as entertaining as Taiwan or Montreal and Dale agreed.

"Boston is pretty quiet," said Dale, "more like Toronto, but I'll take you to my favorite restaurant here, Legal Seafood."

It was a good choice. They started with two dozen raw oysters and large mugs of Sam Adams Boston Lager, then returned to the surf-and-turf preference they had established in Las Vegas. They both ordered a half-pound broiled lobster with an eight-ounce medium-rare New York steak.

The next morning, Dale wanted to visit a few computer stores to check their planned pricing against the competition, then hit the road in the afternoon and be home for the early evening. Sammy had other plans.

"Before we leave," Sammy said, "I need to get a haircut."

"Sammy, you'll be very disappointed," said Dale. "It'll be some fat Boston-Irish or Italian guy and it'll be just a haircut."

"Oh no," said Sammy, "I phoned a friend in Taiwan last night who does business in Boston and he gave me the name of this place."

He showed Dale a page from the hotel notepad where he had written *Ivy's Oriental Massage Parlor* with an address and a phone number.

"I made an appointment for us at four o'clock."

Oh shit, this guy is going to get me in trouble, one way or another.

"OK Sammy, take a break if you really need it, but it's not for me and I've got to get back to Montreal as soon as we can. I'll wait for you and do some work in the car."

Later, on the drive back to Montreal in the dark, they had time to discuss more details of their joint venture in New England. Sammy was optimistic. He relaxed and reclined the seat back to doze off.

Dale kept his eyes on the road ahead and watched the headlights pass over the trees along the side of the road. He was well aware of the hazard of a moose or deer jumping out of the dark onto the highway.

The car phone rang and Dale quickly picked it up. It was Frank.

"Hey Dale, where are you?"

Dale explained he had to make a quick trip to Boston with Sammy, who was now asleep beside him on the way home.

"Well, don't waste any time," said Frank. "We need to get moving on our plan before Boncanno and his henchmen decide to act first."

"OK," said Dale, "I'll get on it first thing tomorrow. Try to keep an eye on them until we can set it up. I'll call Susan now to be sure there's no sign of them around the house again and make sure she's safe."

He tried not to drive any faster in the dark, but thoughts of his family unprotected at home pushed his foot closer to the floor.

30.

André Lebeau was sitting at his kitchen table looking at reports from his three stores and trying to re-balance inventory. He crushed a cigarette butt into the overflowing ashtray and pushed his hand through his long hair to get it out of his eyes. The phone rang. He reached for it at the end of a twisted spiral cord that stretched from the wall across the table and under some newspapers.

"*Oui?*"

It was the store clerk downstairs telling him that Dale Hunter from 3D Computers was on the line. André looked confused, he thought Hunter had been avoiding him.

"*Bonjour*, Dale," he said.

"*Bonjour André, comment ça va?* I promised to call you back after you phoned a few weeks ago. I just got back from COMDEX, so now I have some news for you."

There was a pause before André replied.

"OK, what's new?"

"Listen, André, I think we have some issues we should settle before we do business again. I'd like us to meet. There are some things we need to fix and I'm sure we can sort it out. What do you think?"

"Not sure I know what you're talking about, Dale."

"OK, let me be more specific. I understand you may be working with Gino Boncanno. I know he's a little upset with me and maybe you are too. I can't do anything about Boncanno, that bridge has been crossed and burned behind us. But I'd prefer you and I sort it out and not hold any grudges. We don't have to agree on how we do business, but we can still do business."

Dale paused and let André digest this change of tone. He wondered if it sounded convincing.

"*Daccord, ça me semble une bonne idée,*" said André. "Seems like a good idea, Dale, maybe we can try again. When can you come here?"

"Actually André, I would like us to get off to a good start by buying you dinner. How about Roosters Brasserie in old Montreal on Tuesday evening after work?"

André knew the restaurant and on a Tuesday evening there would be almost no one else there.

"*Excellent*, I like that spot. Tuesday at seven will be fine," he said.

"Great, see you then," said Dale.

After hanging up, André reached for another cigarette. He lit it, took a long draw and exhaled a cloud of smoke above the table.

He reached for the phone and dialed Gino Boncanno.

"Gino, *mon ami*," he said, "I think we can make your plan work after all."

He told Gino about the meeting arranged with Hunter and they agreed, this was the opportunity they were waiting for.

"Come over for lunch tomorrow," Gino said, "We'll sit with Jonnie to finalize the plan."

***

Dale had just phoned Frank to tell him about the conversation with Lebeau and he was pacing nervously in his office.

He reached for the chair to sit down at his conference table and start signing the checks that Monique had placed there for him. He stopped and pushed the chair back, then grabbed his jacket and headed out to the parking lot. He needed to go for a drive.

The BMW veered roughly onto the street and turned hard left toward Fifty-Fifth Avenue accelerating to catch the green light and then screeching south toward Highway 20.

Damn, this car feels good when I drive it hard.

The lights were red at the underpass and Dale braked late. The car crouched smoothly to a stop like a cat ready to pounce when the lights changed green. When they did, he turned sharply right to roar up the ramp and rocket into the right-hand lane on Highway 20 West toward Dorval Airport. He checked the side mirror then hammered the accelerator and slung the car into the far left lane as he shifted into fifth, then sixth and raced by the other traffic. He took the curved overpass above Dorval Circle at ninety-five, then downshifted quickly to exit at Sources Road and go up the ramp to loop over the highway and come back again. He caught the green light and whipped around the traffic circle to go down Cote-de-Liesse, then south again on Fifty-Fifth. Two right turns and he was back in his parking lot at 3D Computers.

I needed that.

The checks to sign were still waiting for him on the conference table in his office.

31.

Roosters Brasserie was in Old Montreal in a row of tall old commercial buildings opposite the docks and attractions of the Old Port. In the summertime, the area was busy with tourists visiting the souvenir shops, patio restaurants and bars, but in the dark evening of early winter, the area was nearly deserted.

The brasserie was in a sturdy grey stone building that had been an armoury two hundred years ago and had been converted into a restaurant and bar in the past decade. The space was unusual in that it consisted of several small rooms with thick stone walls and small doorways originally designed to reduce the risk of an accidental explosion destroying the armoury. There was a broad room at the far end of the restaurant with small tables in front of a large bar which ran along the stone wall behind it. The dining area consisted of several small rooms off the narrow hallway that ran from the street entrance to the bar. It was an awkward layout for the waiters, but comfortably private for the diners in each room.

When Dale arrived, shortly after six, there was a table with four young people sitting in a small dining room to the left, enjoying their drinks and dinner, oblivious to Dale and their surroundings. A tall gentleman was seated in a dark corner of the lounge at the far end of the bar. He was wearing a long topcoat with the collar turned up and a peaked wool winter cap pulled low over his eyes. Obviously, he preferred to drink alone. There was a bartender wiping glasses and one idle waiter leaning on the bar next to him. Chattering and clattering came from the kitchen entrance beside the other end of the bar.

Dale sat at a small table in the lounge in front of the bar, ordered a *Labatt Bleu* beer and waited for André Lebeau. He wore an open brown suede leather jacket over a bulky blue wool sweater.

Lebeau arrived about six-thirty and seemed surprised to see Dale already there.

"Let's take a table in here," said Dale, picking up his beer glass and indicating the small room back down the hallway away from the other diners. It had a heavy square table and four wooden armchairs around it.

"We can be more private here and enjoy our meal."

"Perfect," said André.

They ducked through the low framed doorway and went in. The waiter followed them. He presented the large red leather menus and took André's order for another *Labatt Bleu*. Dale started browsing his menu with one eye on André and watched him set his briefcase beside the chair then remove his coat and lay it over the empty chair between them.

Dale was unaware of Jacques Talbot, who had come in quietly and slipped into the first small room near the front door, taking a seat with his back to the doorway. Talbot leaned back and tried to listen to the conversation between Dale and Lebeau in the room two doors down the hall, but couldn't make out what they were saying.

Talbot slipped his right hand into his coat pocket and gripped Lebeau's small handgun. In the left pocket he had another handgun that he intended to get Hunter's finger prints onto before leaving it at the scene. He wore thin leather gloves on both hands.

A waiter appeared in the doorway.

"*Bonsoir, monsieur,*" he said and offered Jacques a menu. "*Voulez-vous quelque chose à boire?*"

Jacques took the menu and laid it on the table.

"*Non, merci. Je vais attendre.*"

The waiter left him alone after Jacques declined anything to eat or drink. He listened intently to the faint conversation between Dale and André Lebeau coming from the other dining room.

The tall gentleman had left the bar and was sitting peering at the menu in the lounge area on the other side of the wall from where Dale and Lebeau were seated. He was still hidden in his long overcoat and winter cap.

The table of four were settling their bill with the waiter at the bar and preparing to leave.

Dale and André Lebeau were sipping their beers and straining to make polite conversation. The waiter came in to ask if they were ready to order and they replied simultaneously, "*Pas encore, merci.* No, not yet."

As the waiter left, André reached below the table and Dale nervously watched him pull a thick brown envelope out of his briefcase and lay it on the table.

"What's this?" said Dale.

André lifted the open envelope and dumped the bundles of cash onto the table. He looked intently at Dale.

"This is the cash you came here to steal."

Before Dale could respond, Lebeau jumped up knocking over his chair and yelled loudly.

"No, no, Mr. Hunter, please don't shoot! I'll give you the money. Help! Help!"

Dale stood up and leaned on the table.

"André, calm down! What the hell are you doing?"

Suddenly, the looming figure of Jacques Talbot appeared at the low doorway and he stepped into the room. Dale saw he was pointing a small handgun at him and holding another in his left hand.

"You're dead, Hunter," said Talbot.

In the same instant, the tall gentleman came like a dark pouncing panther through the door behind Talbot. Frank the Fixer, without his overcoat or winter cap, slammed his forearm hard into the back of Talbot's neck. Talbot collapsed with a groan and the two guns clattered to the floor.

Dale backed against the wall behind him and André Lebeau moved away from the table and stared at Frank.

"Who are you?"

"Hello, André. I'm this guy's worst nightmare," said Frank, poking his toe into Talbot's ribs and placing his foot on his throat.

He nodded towards Dale.

"And this guy's guardian angel. Listen to me, André. This has to end now."

Lebeau was very still and wide-eyed.

Frank leaned down and scooped up the two handguns. Holding the small pistol he looked at André.

"Is this yours?"

André nodded slowly.

"And you were going to use it on my friend here, right?"

"No, not me, him," said Lebeau gesturing to Talbot on the floor, without taking his eyes off Frank.

"OK," said Frank, "Let's use it on him instead."

He slammed the guns on the table, reached down for Talbot and lifted him roughly onto Dale's empty chair letting him flop forward face-first onto the table. Then he picked up Lebeau's pistol and offered it to him.

"OK, now shoot him."

Lebeau was pale and trembling.

"*Non, non, je peux pas*, I cannot. He's a killer, not me."

He raised his hands in surrender. Frank took one stride toward him, grabbed his right hand and wrapped it around the pistol grip.

"It's easy," he said.

Pointing the barrel at Talbot, he pulled the trigger.

The shot was stunningly loud in the small stone-walled room. Talbot's body jerked and a wet red stain appeared on his right thigh. He moaned again and slid further onto the table.

Dale jumped toward the door and yelled.

"Jesus! Frank, what're you doing?"

Frank put his hand on Lebeau's chest and pushed him hard against the wall.

"There you go, André, you wanted to shoot the robber and now you did. We're going to leave before the police arrive and you are going to deliver a message to your boss, Gino Boncanno. First, remind him Frank the Fixer warned him not to try to hurt my friend here. Second, tell him he'll now be receiving a visit from some friends of mine. He knows who that is."

He pushed Talbot off the table and back to the floor, where he slumped in a heap, still unconscious. Frank made sure he was still out with a hard kick in the ribs that elicited another groan, then he stepped up to the table and pushed the cash back in the envelope.

"Thanks for looking after our expenses," he said, as he tucked the envelope under his arm and scowled at Lebeau.

Frank nodded to Dale to leave. He looked back at Lebeau again.

"You clear on the messages?"

"*Oui monsieur*," was the quick reply, "Yes sir, Frank the Fixer."

"We should go out the back through the kitchen," Dale said.

Frank grabbed his arm, reached for his coat and hat and pushed him toward the front door. He looked back at the bartender and a waiter crouched behind the bar. Another waiter looked out from the kitchen.

"We don't need any more staff describing us to the police. Keep your head down and move it."

They went out to the street and turned immediately right, away from the approaching sirens and walked quickly down the broad sidewalk. It appeared nobody outside had taken any notice of the noise and commotion inside the old stone armoury.

Dale drove Frank back to where he had parked the Caddy.

"Dammit Frank, you nearly got me killed back there. First Talbot wants to take a shot at me and shows up with two guns to be sure of it. Then you take a shot that almost hits me, instead of him."

"Come on, Dale. We were prepared for some rough stuff. You were wearing that Kevlar vest I got you from Hélène Bourassa, right? Nothing to worry about. I think we convinced them to leave you alone now."

"Yeah, well you're used to this violent shit with guns and the rest, not me. Next time I want a gun myself, not just a Kevlar vest."

Frank looked at Dale and shook his head.

"I don't use guns, Dale. Didn't you notice? It's usually the shooter that gets hurt with the gun. There won't be a next time anyway, we're done with these guys. That's the end of it."

"OK, I hope Somalia style works and it's finally over. But what about Gino? If he's behind this, he'll just try again now. How do we stop him permanently?"

"Don't worry about Gino, he's about to get shut down for good. I'll see the Renaldis tonight and we'll take care of him. You won't have to worry about Gino anymore."

Dale was hoping Frank was right.

He was ready to get back to business without any more hassles from these assholes. He didn't give a damn what they did to Boncanno. He deserved all the damage the Renaldis could do to him.

***

Two days later, Dale read in the *Journal de Montréal* about a settling of accounts in Montréal Nord.

The restaurant Luna Rossa had been fire-bombed and part of the reception hall at the Club Calabrese had been badly damaged. The neighbours had reported gunshots and one victim had been found dead in the rubble. His name was Vito D'Alessandro, apparently well-known to the police. He had suffered both burns and gunshot wounds.

There was no news on the status or the whereabouts of the presumed owner, Mr. Gino Boncanno.

32.

In early spring, the dirty piles of melting snow covered in sand and salt pushed to the edges of the parking lot did not improve the view from Dale's office. The small patch of grass between the parking lot and the sidewalk was still brown.

Dale was leaning back in the swivel chair with his heels resting on the corner of the desk, hands behind his head. He was not entirely comfortable in that pose. *But this feels right for a successful businessman, big-shot international executive, widely-admired entrepreneur and secret crime-buster extraordinaire.*

OK, OK, let's not get too carried away. He smiled to himself. *But it's good to be focused on running the business again, instead of trying to avoid the crime and violence the local gangsters were throwing at me.*

It had been several months without any more news of Jacques Talbot or Gino Boncanno. The Renaldis were still getting their protection money and seemed to be content with the arrangement. Dale had not heard from Frank or Forsey and hoped everyone had moved on to other business.

He looked out at the setting sun flashing in orange streaks off the windows across the street and wondered again if any of those businesses had ever been drawn to the criminal side.

He saw several trucks in their parking lots, but no Dodge Ram pickup that he recognized.

***

In the dusk on St. Catherine Street, the brightly lit interior of *InfoCité* stood out in the row of dull rundown retail shops.

A Midland Courier delivery van was double-parked at the front door and the driver had wheeled his hand-truck up to the cashier with two large cartons on it. He was holding out some paperwork for the pimply teenager behind the counter. The kid looked at it, said something to the other store clerk, and then gestured to the driver that he would take the paperwork upstairs to André Lebeau.

He went out by the side door and as he turned to go up the stairs toward André's apartment, he saw a heavy tough-looking man with a bad limp, rushing down. The man's hand went up to cover his face and he avoided eye contact as he brushed by and quickly exited to the street.

The kid frowned at him, shrugged and then took long, lanky strides, two-at-a-time up the stairs. He was thinking, *that guy's been here before. He's never very friendly and he always leaves André in a bad mood.*

He slowed at the landing and cautiously looked down the hall into the apartment. He saw André sitting at the kitchen table with his back to the door. Not wrapped in his ugly green fleecy bathrobe, but wearing a bold checkered green-and-beige sport jacket. His white shirt was pulled awkwardly up above the collar. He seemed unusually still with his head dropped forward.

As the kid approached, he noticed papers on the floor near the table and a small handgun lying below André's dangling right hand. He slid along the wall to look at André from the front.

"*Tabarnac!*" he exclaimed.

Lebeau's head was slumped forward and his white shirt was soaked in blood leaking from a red tear on his chest. The kid jumped back, bumped into the wall and ran quickly back down the stairs, yelling.

"Appelez la Police! Appelez la Police! André est mort!"

He was at the bottom running into the store to call 9-1-1 before wondering maybe André wasn't dead, but he was not going back upstairs. The 9-1-1 operator said dispatch would send the police immediately, so he went and sat on the bottom steps leading upstairs and waited.

Two police cars came quickly with lights flashing and sirens whooping. They pulled up behind the Midland Courier van and the four male officers got out. They wore blue uniforms with heavy protective vests and guns strapped in their holsters. As they came through the front door, the kid pointed them up the stairs. A few minutes later, two officers came back down. One looked at the kid and took out his notepad.

"You the one who phoned it in?"

The kid nodded and the officer started asking questions and taking notes. The other cop went back to the car and picked up the radio.

A few minutes later, an ambulance arrived followed by an unmarked police car with dash lights flashing and no sirens. Hélène Bourassa stepped out of the car onto the sidewalk and a tall young man got out of the driver's side and followed her to the entrance. They wore business suits, not uniforms. They went in calmly and climbed the stairs, observing the staff and customers looking at them from the store.

A crowd was starting to gather on the street and the Midland Courier driver had put his boxes back in the truck. He was standing on the sidewalk waiting to ask the police if he could leave the scene.

***

It was late at 3D Computers and everyone had left the office except Dale. He was reviewing print-outs he had brought back from Boston. A file folder was opened on the blotter in front of him, other files were arranged neatly on the side of his desk. His chin was in his left hand as he scanned the document and circled some numbers with his ball point.

The office phone rang at reception and Dale saw the line flashing at his desk. He picked it up and answered, wondering who would be expecting anyone there at this time of night.

"*Bonsoir,* 3D Computer Products, good evening. Can I help you?"

He was surprised to hear the voice of Detective Pierre Forsey.

"Hello, Dale, your wife told me you were still at the office. Haven't you made enough money yet to take a little time off once in a while?"

"The work's never done, Pierre. How about yourself, working so late."

He hadn't heard from Forsey for months. Dale had long ago lost confidence in him and preferred working with Frank to look after his problems with criminals. Forsey had been worse than useless and Dale still suspected he was on the take.

"I assume this is not a social call."

"No, but I may have some good news for you," said Pierre.

Dale sat back and waited to hear what this was all about.

"I understand you had some trouble a few months ago with André Lebeau and Jonnie Talbot at Roosters in Old Montreal."

Damn.

Dale had hoped he would never hear those names again. And it was not good news that Forsey knew so much. He and Frank must be keeping in touch and probably still doing business together, too.

"I don't know what you're talking about," Dale said. "Never been there."

"Yeah, OK, that's the right answer, I guess. Anyway, I thought you might like to know that Lebeau is dead and we're bringing in Talbot tonight to be charged with his murder."

Dale was stunned into silence and didn't reply, so Forsey continued with a few details about André's body being found at *InfoCité* and Talbot being picked up in his apartment after being identified from a mug shot by the kid at the store.

"I thought you might want to come down here and help us put some pressure on your old friend, Jacques,' said Forsey. "Maybe we can get a confession out of him."

"But you just told me that you have an eye-witness and you found him with a bloody switchblade in the pocket of his coat. That should be enough to nail him for murder. Why do you need me?"

"Well, he's not going to be too quick to cough up a confession to murder, even if he does seem a little rattled and shook up by the whole thing. He was sitting in his apartment staring at the TV and hadn't even tried to clean up or get rid of the blade. Or get the hell out of town."

"I still don't see what you need from me. I don't want to set myself up for more trouble from these guys. They've already tried to kill me once and they've threatened my family. We know what they're capable of."

"Look, Dale, we'll keep you out of it. He'll never know you're here. But I thought you'd like to help put him away for as long as we can."

"I would," said Dale, wondering if it would bring any real satisfaction.

He hesitated, as Pierre waited.

"OK, I'll be there in half an hour."

But now I'll have to explain to Susan that this never-ending story continues and I hope I'm not putting us in danger all over again.

***

Station 21 was in a plain white brick and concrete block building of six stories on Boulevard de Maisonneuve west of downtown. Above the wide glass front door was an illuminated white sign with bold blue letters, POLICE *Poste de quartier 21 - Service de police de la Ville de Montréal.*

Several blue and white police cars were on the street in front. Dale parked behind the building. He walked in the front door and asked at the counter for Detective Forsey. He looked around at the other visitors sitting in the worn wooden chairs and wondered what their stories might be. The walls were covered with billboards and notices, French predominant, the English in much smaller letters. It was quiet there now, but probably not often.

Forsey came around the corner and they shook hands.

"Thanks for coming in, Dale. Let's go to my office."

They went back around the corner and down the hall to a closed office with two framed glass windows covered from inside by closed Venetian blinds. Pierre walked in and closed the door, indicating a chair for Dale in front of his desk as he squeezed past and slumped into the creaking wooden armchair behind it.

"I want to see him," Dale said.

Forsey's eyebrows went up.

"I thought you didn't want him to know you were here."

"I changed my mind," said Dale. "I haven't seen the sonofabitch since he tried to kill me and I don't want him to think I'm intimidated or hiding from him. I want him to know you have everything you need to put him away and I helped you do it."

"OK, let's do that," said Forsey with a grin.

They left Forsey's office and went further down the hall and around another corner to approach a narrow undecorated room with two people sitting opposite Jacques Talbot at a four-legged metal table. They looked in through the steel bars at the wide window.

Talbot was looking down at his handcuffed hands. Dale didn't know the two detectives. One was a petite brunette in a dark blue pantsuit and plain white blouse. Her pretty face was locked in stern determination. Beside her was an eager young man in a grey suit and pale blue shirt with a multi-colored paisley tie pulled loose from his neck. He was leaning across the table and speaking animatedly to Talbot.

"Who are those two?" asked Dale.

"The cute little lady is Hélène Bourassa from homicide and the rookie, full of piss and vinegar as they say, is Paul Carney. They are working together for a few months until Hélène transfers to her next gig in organized crime. As you know, Lebeau was dirty and doing business with these guys for a long time."

"Yeah, he was no sweetheart. But he didn't deserve this ugly ending."

Talbot looked up and saw them standing outside the window. Dale gave him a hard stare.

Hey you bastard, it's time you got what you deserve and I'm here to make it happen.

Jacques looked back at him blankly, then focused and frowned at Dale, before turning again to the detectives.

"OK, that'll do," said Dale, "Let's go back to your office and finish this."

Back in Forsey's office, Dale confirmed what Forsey already knew about the incident at Roosters where Talbot and Lebeau had set up to kill him, until Frank intervened.

"I told you Frank was good, eh?"

"Yeah, he saved my ass. Talbot was definitely there with murder on his mind. What happened between him and André Lebeau? I thought they were partners in crime working for Gino Boncanno."

"Well, something went wrong. That's what they're trying to find out in there."

Back in the interview room, they had told Jacques about the eye witness, exaggerating just a little about what they actually knew. They did not mention Dale Hunter, but they too had seen him looking in on them and had noted Jacques' reaction. They wanted to squeeze a confession for murder out of him, but he was claiming self-defence, knowing that nobody had actually seen what happened.

"The slimy little prick pulled a gun on me, so I stuck a shiv in his chest, before he could pull the trigger."

"Boncanno send you to settle some accounts and Lebeau wasn't co-operating?" asked Hélène.

"Who's Boncanno?"

"Right. Working on your own again were you, Jacques?"

Hélène was well aware of his history and had shared most of it with Paul Carney.

"Listen, you're being charged with murder, so you better give some serious thought to telling us the whole story. Think about it. We'll be back after we talk to another witness."

Jacques looked back out the window where he had seen Dale and then directed his eyes back to the table. The two officers got up, attached one of his handcuffs to the iron ring in the centre of the table and left him alone.

They walked down to Forsey's office to join Pierre and Dale. Paul Carney leaned against the wall beside the desk and Hélène sat with legs crossed in the chair beside Dale. She thanked him for coming in and Dale thought Frank was right, cute, but tough.

She turned to Pierre.

"Maybe we can offer him a deal, if he'll rollover on Boncanno."

Pierre looked skeptical.

"You're pretty terrifying Hélène, but I think he's more afraid of Boncanno. He'll never mention his name."

Dale leaned in to look at Hélène.

"I can tell you how he tried to kill me, if that helps."

Hélène was even prettier, when she smiled.

"Well, I think he got the message through the window all right. Thanks for letting him know you're working with us. It helps us when the victim cooperates."

Dale flinched at the idea he was a victim.

"These guys are bad bastards, so I'm glad to help put them out of business, if I can. What about Boncanno, have you nailed him yet?"

Hélène stopped smiling.

"We're working on it."

Looks were exchanged between the three detectives. Dale checked his watch.

"Well, if you don't need me anymore," he said, "It's late and I'd like to go home."

"We're good for now," said Forsey, "I'll be in touch if we need you again."

Great, this is never going to end, thought Dale.

When he got home from the police station, Susan was already in bed and trying to sleep. Dale decided the news could wait until morning, so he crawled in and quickly fell asleep himself.

***

The next morning, he was up before Susan, but still at the breakfast table after the kids had taken the school bus and left for the day.

"You taking a day off, Dale?" Susan asked, when she came into the kitchen.

"Nope, but I was thinking a little afternoon delight before breakfast would be good. The kids are away, I thought we could play."

She laughed at him.

"Dream on, buster. I've got a busy day ahead of me."

"That's OK, we can be quick. I have to get to the office soon too. You can be late for tennis." He flicked his eyebrows playfully and attempted an alluring smile.

"I already cancelled tennis. I got a call from palliative care and they need me to fill in for another volunteer, who can't make it today. And I don't see any flowers or a bottle of wine, either."

"Jeez, you didn't use to be so difficult."

"Yeah? You didn't used to be so distracted all the time. What's going on now, Dale? More bad news?"

"Nope, nothing but good news. All our troubles are over. Boncanno is still shut down and now Talbot's going to jail. Finally we can get back to our quiet happy lives. So let's celebrate somehow. How about I make you a nice breakfast, if you're not up for some morning delight?"

"You're on your own," she said, shaking her head. "I'm leaving in five minutes."

"OK, I'll make myself something. But it's a good plan for another day, don't you think? I'll remember to bring flowers and wine and give you five minutes notice next time."

She laughed and smacked him on the shoulder as he went to the fridge.

33.

That afternoon, Detective Forsey was with Gino Boncanno tucked into a corner at the back of a nearly empty Italian restaurant in Saint Léonard. It was not far from the Luna Rossa, which had not yet re-opened. Gino was looking tired, dejected and subdued. He pushed the pasta around his plate, before each mouthful.

Forsey looked in charge, this time.

"Gino, this is a problem. I can't protect you if you start killing people."

"Not my fault. Jonnie lost control of the situation. And he doesn't work for me anyway."

"Don't worry, he's being very careful not to use your name. He'd rather go to jail than piss you off again. A good lawyer may even get him off first-degree down to manslaughter. Even self-defence. You must know a good lawyer."

"His problem."

"What about Hunter?" Forsey asked.

Gino looked at him darkly and chewed slowly, before replying.

"I've had enough of him for now. He keeps messing things up for us. Let's leave him alone for a while."

Gino had decided to keep out of sight and had not yet re-established his organization or his business activities. He was staying away from home and living with his brother in Ville Saint Laurent. He had moved his family to a cottage on the lake near Mont Tremblant about an hour-and-a-half north of Montreal.

He was still trying to decide when and how to get back into his old rackets without causing the Renaldis to come back and finish him off. Maybe he needed to arrange a summit meeting like the Americans and the Russians were doing to make a peace deal.

He was tired of Forsey getting on his nerves with these arrogant little lectures. Giving him orders, instead of doing as he was told and shutting up about it. Gino would have to show him again someday soon, who was really in charge.

***

Dale was having a beer with Frank on the patio deck of the St. Antoine Pub beside the Lachine Canal. They lounged comfortably in the warm spring sunshine.

"Life is good, eh, Dale," said Frank. "Business is booming in Montreal and Boston, no more bad guys giving you a hard time, happy family and a warm sunny summer day. What more could you ask?"

"True enough, everything's good," Dale nodded, "But it could always be better."

He had visited Rick Petrie at the bank that afternoon before going to the pub.

"Typical of banks," said Dale, "whenever I really need them, some idiot in his ivory tower in Toronto checks the computer and says, no. My account manager here is a good guy, but he can't change it to a yes. Bunch of tight-ass bureaucrats, they'll never understand what drives an entrepreneur."

"Do you?" Frank asked.

"Of course, we're all in it just for the money."

Dale laughed and took a long sip of his beer.

"Nah, I can't explain it either," he said. "We're all a little nuts and stubbornly independent beyond all reason. Anyway, now that I don't need the bank, they'll give me whatever I want. Well, almost. They're finally ready to increase my credit line, so I can keep growing sales, but still according to their terms, not mine."

"Better than Renaldi's terms at Ottimo, I bet," said Frank. "How're you doing with that crazy Chinaman you took on as partner?"

Frank reached for the basket of fries and pulled one out, looking disgusted at the greasy brown strip of potato, before putting it in his mouth.

"How's that working out for you?"

Dale thought for a minute about Boston, as he pulled the basket back and placed it exactly in the middle of the round table. He took a fry for himself and another sip of beer.

"We're OK for now. The business in Boston is growing pretty fast too and I'm happy with the results so far. But Sammy has some ideas that will be a problem and I'll have to say, no. That might not go over so well."

"Is he holding back on the money he promised?"

"No, no, he's pretty quick to throw more money at the problem, anytime we need it. But he's also pretty quick to play outside the rules and he makes me nervous sometimes."

"Well, if you need to go back to Ottimo, you better do it soon. Our friend, Hélène Bourassa has been transferred to organized crime and she'll be going after them to shut it down."

"Good for her. Don't worry, I hope I never need them again."

"By the way, she agreed she's not investigating you or me, in spite of her suspicions about us doing dirty deeds together."

"Great," said Dale, "I really wouldn't want to share a jail cell with any of our old friends."

"Oh yeah, I don't want to be there, either. But I need you to get in some trouble, Dale, otherwise I don't have much to do. No work, no moolah. Maybe I should try something new. You still have that sales job for me?"

"Jesus! That's not gonna happen. I have seen enough of your tactics to know my customers would be complaining about you all the time. Go beat up a few more criminals for Forsey, instead."

"All right. You stick to your business and I'll stick to mine."

"That's definitely a better plan," said Dale. They grinned at each other and clinked beer glasses to seal the deal.

And everybody went back to business as usual.

Until the next unplanned interruption.

NEXT IN THE DALE HUNTER SERIES:

SIMPLY THE BEST

"It may be simple, but it's never easy."

by Delvin R. Chatterson

COMING SOON

For your introduction to the next novel by Delvin Chatterson, following is the 1st Chapter from the current manuscript for SIMPLY THE BEST. Please note that the final published edition scheduled for September 2018 may differ from this sample.

1. MEMORIES FROM A HAT

"Jeez Dad, that hat must be thirty years old."

Dale Hunter's son Sean was looking into the front hall closet at a baseball cap hanging on a hook at the back wall.

Dale was living alone in a high-rose condo in the downtown residential suburb of Nun's Island and they were on their way out for dinner together. Sean had just arrived and was reaching into the closet to hang up his jacket, when he saw the hat. It had once been a bright neon orange color, but it had now faded to a pale memory of its original brilliance. It retained the black stitched logo *STB* above the peak with *Simply the Best* written beneath it.

"Yeah, it does go back thirty years. STB was one of our video card suppliers at 3D Computers," said Dale, remembering the company from Texas and their sales rep who got so excited by the strippers in Montreal. He had insisted on going to *Chez Paris* at lunch time, as well as most of the evenings, whenever he was in town.

Whatever it took to do the deal, Dale thought, and it wasn't that much of a hardship. Not like the three or four long days of hospitality and partying around negotiating sessions in Korea and Taiwan, whenever he visited his suppliers there, that was just too exhausting. Even if he was thirty years younger, then.

Dale knew the *STB* hat was hanging there as a souvenir from his days in the computer business and he liked the slogan, *Simply the Best.*

He glanced down the hallway at Sean and called back to him.

"That's the hat I wore for all my marathons, back in the 90s. The fluorescent orange made it easy to find me in the crowd, remember?"

"Yeah, we knew you were never gonna be found at the front of the pack."

"Hey, a little respect for the old man. I didn't do that bad for starting marathons in my 40s. At least I was never last. Hell, in New York there were nine thousand runners who finished behind me."

"Yeah, and twenty-five thousand ahead of you."

"OK smart-ass, you force me to remind you that you were never that fast either, even as a teenager. Dead last in a 10-kilometre race one spring, I remember."

"Yup, that's me, built for power, not for speed."

Sean was now a solid, strongly built thirty-eight year-old and had been on the offensive line for the Concordia University Stingers football team. He had loved to run into people and hit them hard. Otherwise, he was the same studious, gentle personality that he had been as a boy.

"So who was STB, anyway," he said.

"They were one of our better suppliers for video cards actually, very good about supporting us and not too demanding on quotas to maintain exclusivity. We did pretty well with them."

"Good slogan, *Simply the Best*."

"Yeah, I like it too, simple and memorable."

"So they were among the good guys from the old days?"

"Yeah, no real horror stories for STB, they were pretty straightforward."

"I don't remember any horror stories at all," said Sean. "Seems to me, it was all good times in your business back then. Life at home was pretty good too, as I remember."

Yeah, well you didn't hear all the stories, thought Dale.

I never explained all the disruptions from the gangsters and criminals in Montreal that interfered with the business. And we never told you or your sister how they tried to kill me and kidnap your mother.

"Maybe someday I'll tell you the stories of what was really going on back then," he said out loud. "Hopefully you already know enough to manage your own business career. Your biggest challenge at UbiSoft will be navigating the corporate politics inside a big multinational software developer."

"It's no fun putting up with all that crap," Sean replied. "I'd just like to do the work and have some fun. And get paid well for doing it, of course. I'm not yet ready to take off on my own and become an evil entrepreneur, like you. Maybe with a little more experience, then I can start-up my own company in software development."

"That sounds like a better idea than my adventures in computer hardware distribution. It's always a tough challenge when you're a distributor, managing to stay between the supplier and the customer without getting screwed by either one of them. If you ever do go into business for yourself, stay away from the distribution business."

Dale's mind flashed back over memories of his own challenges from customers in Montreal and suppliers in Korea and Taiwan, while he was trying to grow his business in the 1980s.

"Avoid being the middleman if you can. It's much better to have your own product. You'll always have more control over your destiny if you have a unique product that you can conquer the world with. That's what my friend, K.Y. Ho, did at ATI. He started from zero at about the same time as me, but he went on to build ATI into a world leader in graphics cards for computers and was able to exit at fifty-five, after selling his company for five billion."

"Jeez Dad, and all you're got to show for exiting your business is an old hat from STB!"

"Sorry, I would've liked to have had that happy ending, too. It'd be nice to retire with that kind of cash in the bank. So there's another story and another lesson you'll hear someday."

Maybe we settled for making a little less money, but at least we survived. A brief shudder shook his shoulders as he remembered the phone call that had shaken him so badly that afternoon, over thirty years ago.

He was in his office at 3D Computer Products and the call was from his wife at home, but then he heard a gruff man's voice on the line.

"Listen to your wife, Hunter. Just do as you're told and nobody gets hurt."

It wasn't that simple.

***

SYNOPSIS: SIMPLY THE BEST

Dale Hunter is back in business, but so is Gino Boncanno.

Hunter is a young entrepreneur running a successful business in Montreal and Boston in the 1980s world of personal computers. He's having fun, making money and taking good care of his family again, after fighting off the bad guys that had been threatening him and his family. He was able to avoid disaster and a murder attempt by the gangster, Gino Boncanno, who was driven out of business by the Montreal Mafia and Dale's new friend Frank the Fixer. Boncanno has never forgiven Dale for escaping his lucrative protection scam and shutting him down.

While fighting off the gangsters and protecting his family, Dale also had to manage the challenges from his employees, customers and suppliers from Taiwan and Korea to Montreal. His new partner in Boston, Sammy Wong, now introduces Dale to the Triads from Taiwan and their smuggling scheme enforced by more threats of violence. Dale calls on Frank the Fixer to intervene and he brings in his gangster friends in New York to extricate Dale and Sammy from the Triads. The complications and threats of violence escalate.

Frank the Fixer also has to save Dale and his family from the murderous plans of Gino Boncanno back in Montreal. Dale has to deal with them all to stay alive and get back to business as usual.

It should be simple, but it's never easy.

THANK YOU & ACKNOWLEDGEMENTS

Thank you first to all the readers of this novel. Those who read the early versions and encouraged me to keep working on it, and those of you who made it all the way with me to the last page in this final version.

If you just picked it up and accidently flipped to this page, then credit goes to my cover designer for making it jump off the shelf at you. The outstanding covers for these Dale Hunter novels are the work of Caroline Teagle, and they definitely make a good first impression. In spite of that old saying about not judging a book by its cover, I hope this one lives up to your expectations.

My novels and my business books, are all inspired by the real-life stories of the entrepreneurs and business associates that I have worked with during the last thirty years and more. I sincerely thank them all for sharing their stories with me. Some may think they recognize themselves in the characters in the novel, but those are only fictional composites of the real people. My apologies to anyone who may be less than flattered or if I neglected to tell their best stories.

The quality of this novel has also been enhanced by the active support and feedback of my early readers, reviewers and editors, especially friends and family, who cheered me on and inspired me to make it better. They were better than polite, they told me what they really thought of the early draft manuscript and contributed greatly to the success of No Easy Money by reading and reviewing the book, then raving about it and recommending it to their friends. The list of names is too long to print and is *included in the list of supporters at www.DelvinChatterson.com under the Acknowledgements and Thank-you Notes.*

In writing this first book of fiction, I was inspired by the fine work and good advice of many outstanding authors, including John Grisham, John Le Carré, and Ian Rankin, with added instruction for writers from Ernest Hemingway, Stephen King and Sol Stein. In addition, I learned from the expertise of The Wealthy Barber, David Chilton, and business evangelist and best-selling author of A.P.E (Author-Publisher-Entrepreneur), Guy Kawasaki.

The Dale Hunter Series was also inspired by the internationally successful writing of Ian Hamilton with his Ava Lee Novels and Kathy Reichs with her Terrance Brennan series of Bones Novels.

I have benefitted immensely from the competent and experienced support and coaching of my two editors. My great appreciation for their expert guidance goes to Alan Rinzler, for pushing me to a much better manuscript with international appeal, and to Allister Thompson, for keeping me on track and retaining the book's original Canadian authenticity. Together, we finally arrived at the novel you've read in this edition.

Finally, the book design, publishing and distribution were the work of the team of helpful experts at Tellwell Talent. Any remaining deficiencies in the book are all mine and I look forward to feedback from readers and reviewers to make the next book even better.

And to the most important partner in all my projects, I thank my helpful and patient wife, Penny Rankin, who supported, encouraged, challenged, read, reviewed and improved every draft of the novel and loved me through it all.

Thank you!

Del Chatterson

May 2018

A PERSONAL NOTE TO READERS

This novel, the first in a series of Dale Hunter crime thrillers, got started with some wild ideas in my head and some scratchings in a notebook. Two and a half years later, the final manuscript was ready for publication and a series of novels was in process. The stories are based on real business experiences I had as a young entrepreneur, plus some of my worst nightmares, most of which never happened. This is a work of fiction, not a business textbook, not my autobiography. My intent is to make it an interesting and entertaining read with appeal to a wide audience.

I am dedicated to sharing my experience, ideas and advice with entrepreneurs to promote enlightened entrepreneurship and to help entrepreneurs be better and do better, for themselves and their families, their employees, customers and suppliers, their communities and the planet. I am a strategic business advisor, writer, consultant, coach and cheerleader for entrepreneurs. I also try to help promote more sympathy and understanding for entrepreneurs from the many critics and a public that accepts the ugly stereotype of greedy, selfish capitalists.

The theme of sharing stories was used in my two business books, **The Complete Do-It-Yourself Guide to Business Plans** *and* **Don't Do It the Hard Way**. *This theme continues in the dramatic fiction and crime stories of the Dale Hunter Series of novels.*

I hope you enjoy the story, recommend it to your friends, and tell me what I can do to make the next one better. Please contact me at www.DelvinChatterson.com.

Many thanks for your interest in my writing.

Del Chatterson
Montreal, Canada,
May 2018

THE AUTHOR
DEL CHATTERSON

Like Dale Hunter, Del Chatterson is an engineer from UBC with an MBA from McGill and ran a computer products distribution business in Montreal in the 1980s. Some of the stories in his first novel, **No Easy Money**, actually happened, but most are fiction. "These are my worst nightmares," he says, "I decided to share them through these imagined stories."

Del is a strategic advisor, consultant, writer and cheerleader for entrepreneurs and has written extensively on business topics. He is now working on several writing projects, including a short story collection and this series of business novels. He has already published two business books, **Don't Do It the Hard Way**, *A wise man learns from the mistakes of others, only a fool insists on making his own,* and **The Complete Do-It-Yourself Guide to Business Plans**.

Originally from the Rocky Mountains of British Columbia, Del has lived and worked for most of the past forty years in the fascinating, multicultural, bilingual, French-Canadian city of Montreal, Quebec.

Del is dedicated to sharing his ideas, experience and advice with entrepreneurs to help improve their lives and their businesses. He has helped entrepreneurs around the world, including volunteer consulting and financial support in developing economies and in Aboriginal communities. His own life experience includes running nine marathons after the age of fifty (setting no records, but never being last) and running for Member of Parliament in the 2000 Canadian Federal election. (He came second, not last.)

Learn more about Del at his websites www.DelvinChatterson.com and www.LearningEntrepreneurship.com. You may also follow Del on Twitter, Facebook, Instagram or LinkedIn.

Thank you for sharing his books and providing your feedback, comments and reviews. Del welcomes any opportunity to connect with readers.

Made in the USA
Middletown, DE
13 August 2019